SPUR DOUBLE EDITION!
TWICE THE FILLIES! TWICE THE FIGHTIN'!
SAVE $$$!

SALT LAKE LADY

Spur McCoy had heard the talk that someone had shot a halfbreed and ran faster. He had stopped in Logan for supplies with Istas, the half-Ute girl. Now he feared for her life.

He ran ahead of the others and saw several people staring down at a small form lying in the dust of the street. Spur drew his .45 and blasted a shot into the air.

The gawkers around the body pulled back. One man stood, holding a six-gun pointed at the ground. Spur could tell that the man was drunk.

Spur turned to the gunman and was ready to kick him down the block when a small man with a badge pushed through the crowd. The sheriff went over to the man in the dirt, picked up his gun and helped the man stand. He brushed him off, gave him back his gun and talked to him quietly for a minute.

"You're not going to arrest him?" Spur asked.

"Didn't break any law. An Injun isn't a person in Logan," the sheriff told him.

DEADRIDGE DOLL

"Don't move. If you even fart I'll blast you full of lead!" Spur's arms were steady. His fingers teased the trigger of his revolver.

Hardwick raised his ivory right brow. "How can you kill me? I'm legally dead."

"You're standing right there!"

"Yes. They did hang Fancy Freddie Hardwick the day you left St. Louis. It was a drunken bastard my men found on the street. Strange as it might seem, the man looked quite a lot like me." The albino smiled.

"That must have broken his mother's heart," McCoy said.

"Back off, McCoy!" Hardwick said. "This isn't the time. You'll know when it is!"

SPUR

SALT LAKE LADY

DEADRIDGE DOLL

DIRK FLETCHER

LEISURE BOOKS   NEW YORK CITY

A LEISURE BOOK®

October 1995

Published by

Dorchester Publishing Co., Inc.
276 Fifth Avenue
New York, NY 10001

Printed in the United States of America.

SPUR

SALT LAKE LADY

CHAPTER ONE

September 15, 1874—Utah Territory

(Hundreds were injured as the unemployed battled police in New York City. U.S. troops landed in Honolulu to protect the Hawaiian king. Benjamin Disraeli became England's Prime Minister. France assumed protectorate over Vietnam. Germany dissolved the Social Democratic party. Alexander Graham Bell demonstrated his new invention, the electric telephone. Theodore Tilton accused the Reverend Henry Ward Beecher of adultery. The world's first ice cream soda was introduced in Philadelphia by R.M. Green.)

CAPTAIN HARLY LANDOWER, of the 4th Infantry Division, and commander of Company F of the Fifth Cavalry, sat on his black gelding and stared out across ten miles of prime Ute territory. It was high forested country somewhere between the Colorado line and Salt Lake City. The captain was not sure exactly where they were, but they were fulfilling their announced mission: to show the United States flag, and to demonstrate that the army could move in strength anywhere in the Colorado or Utah Territories quickly, and with plenty of men and equipment to fight.

That was the mission of record.

Captain Landower was a slender man about five-ten, with bright red hair and a red moustache. He kept trim, had a wife and two children back at Camp Pilot Butte in Wyoming. They had not seen any Indians so far, but were aware that the redmen knew they were in the area, and passing through.

They had camped just below in a small valley where there was plenty of forage and water for both animals and men. Tonight they would slaughter one of the six steers they had driven with them and the men would gorge themselves on fresh red meat.

Utes! He knew as much about them as any soldier west of the Mississippi. They formed a large and important division of the Shoshonean tribes of Colorado, Utah and New Mexico. And were usually described as "warlike." Which to most whites meant they were hunters and not farmers. They roamed with the game, made raids on unfriendly nearby tribes, and thundered their displeasure at the white men invaders wherever they found them.

Landower reflected on his use of the word "warlike." The white man was definitely the invader. These people had lived on this land for centuries before the Mayflower set sail. Now he was charging through their hunting grounds and their sacred burial grounds like some invading beast from the East.

The Utes were warlike but they were also realistic. Many of the bands and subtribes, under the great chief Ouray, had avoided the Blue Coats. Ouray was known to believe that there was plenty of room for both whites and Indians. He would fight only when he considered that the odds were in his favor. He had seen too many Indian tribes slaughtered by the vicious long guns of the Pony Soldiers. He was a smart tactician and would not be drawn into a war of annihilation, because he knew he would lose.

Captain Landower swung his mount around and worked back down the two hundred yards to the headwaters of the small stream they would use for the Officer Country bivouac.

He had a hundred men below, all well armed, half had been blooded, and most were in good spirits. They did not expect to see any real action on this month-long patrol.

After another six or seven days moving slowly toward Ogden, they would rest for three days and load all animals and equipment on the next train through and return by rail to Camp Pilot Butte a little over a hundred and seventy miles away. At least that's what their official orders said they would do. It could turn out differently.

He cocked his head. Rifle fire? He listened again, but the wind came up causing rustling whispers in the tall pines and the aspens. He listened again, but the wind continued.

Captain Landower swore softly. He had sent Lt. Joseph Windsong out to post pickets as a ring of outer protection. He should be back by now. Landower scowled. If anything happened to Lt. Windsong while under his command, the Landower family could kiss goodbye to his army career. The young lieutenant was the only son of Lieutenant General Hartford Windsong, one of the most respected generals in the army.

Again the faint sound of rifle fire came and Captain Landower called the sergeant of the guard and put the inner guards on alert. His only consolation was that Sgt. Bennedict was with Lt. Windsong. Bennedict was his most experienced non-com. He would pull the officer through if there was a fight.

Sgt. Hirum Bennedict fired his new Springfield breech loading carbine and saw a Ute spin behind a rock and go down. He loaded another round in the single shot Springfield and looked for a new target. He and Lt. Windsong had just positioned one pair of pickets on a little knoll and turned left into this small gully when the Utes hit them. It must have been a hasty ambush, because with some planning and control the Indians could have wiped out the eight men left in the picket posting detail.

Sgt. Bennedict fired again, missed and reloaded. What he wouldn't give right now for a seven shot repeater, even an old Spencer. It would keep the bloody savages down.

Lt. Windsong huddled behind a rock where Sgt. Bennedict had positioned him. The officer had almost broken when he heard the first volley of incoming fire. Sgt. Bennedict had pulled him off his horse and yelled at the men to take cover.

"Sergeant!" Lt. Windsong called.

"Keep your head down or they'll shoot it off, Lieutenant," Bennedict shouted, then fired three times quickly and stopped two Utes who were trying to circle around them.

"Sergeant, I'm getting out of here!" Lt. Windsong screeched. He jumped up and ran toward the horses, which had been caught by the harrier and hurried into the brush behind them.

"No!" Sgt. Bennedict shouted. Bullets whizzed around the running figure. He came toward Bennedict who reared up, grabbed the officer and pulled him down behind the big boulder.

"Let me go, damn you! I'll have you up on charges for striking an officer!"

"You just do that, but you stay here until we get this pack of hyenas driven off."

Lt. Windsong began to shake. He had left his pistol by the other rock. He turned toward the sergeant, and tears gushed out of his eyes. "Please let me go back," he pleaded. His crying increased to a blubbering. "I'm afraid! I can't even stand to hear them shooting! Don't you understand, I'm AFRAID!" Sgt. Bennedict fired his Springfield twice more, then looked at the officer where he slumped in the protection of the granite boulder. As the enlisted man watched, a dark stain appeared at Lt. Windsong's crotch, and then the pungent, unmistakable stench of human feces came through the crisp mountain air.

"Here they come!" someone down the line shouted. The Utes made another rush. Half were on ponies, half slipping from tree to rock.

The troopers laid down a concentrated fire, first knocking down the horses, then punishing the riders now in the open. Slowly the volume of fire from the Utes fell off, as they began to edge to the rear.

The Company F troopers fired faster, driving the last redmen back into the trees and into the next valley.

Two minutes later the firing stopped. Sgt. Bennedict crawled and ran from one group of his men to the next. They had lost two men who had been killed on the first attack, and two wounded afterward. They had held. Quickly Bennedict sent one mounted man to scout the Utes and see how far they had pulled back and to figure out if they would attack again.

Then Sgt. Bennedict marshalled his men, took their dead and wounded, doubled up on horses and made ready to march.

The sergeant looked down at Lt. Wingsong. He was still shivering and shaking. He helped the officer onto his horse, and led the men back toward their camp. New picket guards would go out later.

At the camp, Captain Landower came to meet them. He had been told by one of the pickets who rode in that the detail had been ambushed. As soon as he saw Lt. Windsong he knew what had happened. The man rode like a corpse, eyes downcast, shoulders slumped. Sgt. Bennedict rode up to him, said something and then dismissed the detail. An enlisted man with some medical training rushed up to the wounded men and began treating them.

Captain Landower looked at the officer and sighed. "Windsong, go to your quarters and clean yourself up, then report to my tent."

By the time Lt. Windsong arrived, Captain Landower had talked with Sgt. Bennedict for fifteen minutes. The sergeant left as the officer came in.

"Lies!" Windsong said. "Whatever he told you are lies! I'm putting that soldier on report and filing charges against him for striking a commissioned officer!"

"And you'll include in your report, Lt. Windsong, how you shit your pants when your detail was attacked, and Sgt. Bennedict had to assume command and rally the troops and drive off the hostiles?"

"Lies!"

Captain Landower stood up and stared at the slightly taller man. Then he slapped him hard on the side of the face. The blow knocked down Lt. Windsong. He sat on the floor of the tent, tears gushed from his eyes. He rocked back and forth as he cried.

Captain Landower kicked him in the ass.

"Stand up, damnit!" he roared. "You stand up and act half way like a man, or I'm going to execute you right here for cowardice in the face of the enemy, and endangering your men's lives. I could do it and be within regulations. Now stand up!"

Slowly the officer got to his feet.

"Windsong, you have one more chance. Either you shape up and pull your weight, or you'll never stay in the army, I don't care if your father is the best damn general the army has. Now get out of here. Select new men for picket duty and make sure they are placed at once. Then check the condition of your two wounded, and bury your two dead with appropriate services. Dismissed!"

The captain had just sat down to supper in his tent when a knock sounded on his door.

"Come!"

The man who came in was not in uniform. He wore store bought jeans and an Indian made doeskin, fringed shirt. He saw that the officer was eating, but sat down cross-legged on the floor of the tent.

"You're going to have some real trouble with him one of these days," the civilian said. His name was Lawson Kirk, and he had known Captain Landower for three years, ever since he came to his current assignment. Kirk was the special civilian scout hired for this trip since he knew the country inside out. He was thirty-one years old, wore a trimmed close full beard, showed light blue eyes under sparse brows, and a head of brown hair he kept tied in back like a pony's tail with a rawhide thong.

The captain put down his fork and looked away from the thick, choice, rare-cooked steak.

"Every enlisted man knows exactly what happened out there?"

"True, and wondering what you'll do."

"What do they think?"

"They want you to courtmartial him, but seeing he's an officer the betting is two hundred to one you won't. The officer code and all, which you and I both know is a bunch of bullshit."

Captain Lawson grinned. He knew Kirk too well to get angry. "So what do they think I'll do?"

"Cover up for him like you did the last two times."

"Three times, one the men don't even know about." He went back to the steak. After he ruined half the beef on his plate he looked back at the scout.

"The men know our real mission out here?"

"Is this the army? Sure they know."

The captain sighed. "We are to show the flag, to let the Utes know that we can get into the area in strength within two or three days, and that we can fight when we get here. Then our real mission from Senator Patterson. We are to proceed to the Ute stronghold and there rescue his daughter Priscilla and any other white captives taken on the raid on the undefended train stopped in the mountain water tower this past June 15."

"Sounds like a snap, Captain."

"Sounds that way. The men know about Sadie, too?"

"Yep. This is still the same army. They know my Sadie was on the train too. They know that the

Utes killed six civilians that day, stole twenty horses from a boxcar, and got away clean without even a scratched red backside. They know."

"Figures." He ate the rest of the steak. "You get fed, Kirk?"

"Too much. Everybody eats good next two days." He was quiet for a moment. "Suggestions, Major."

Landower looked up and grinned. It was one of their continuing little games, giving each other promotions.

"Way I see it, we should keep our pickets in closer, post them no more than a hundred yards out. Utes gonna sit out there and wait for another small detail to come with outside pickets, and they gonna hit us again."

"Agreed. Do you think that was Spotted Tail's men, the ones who hit us tonight?"

"Not him, nohow. He's sitting snug in his camp somewhere, eating and playing with his new white bride. Sadie is too young for him, only thirteen. He's the one who helped convince old Ouray that not even the mighty Utes could whip the whole U.S. Army. Way I hear it he thinks there are a million Pony Soldiers out there, just waiting their turn to come in and kill redmen."

"Twenty-four thousand is more like it, and the army is spread out in thirty states and territories."

"How do we find him, Captain?"

"Nail a renegade or two in Ogden who will do anything for a bottle of firewater."

"Illegal as hell."

"Yeah, you going to report me?"

"Not if it works. Hell, right now I'll try anything if it will work. I'd even let Lt. Windsong make captain if he can get me into Spotted Tail's camp."

"And after we get Sadie and the others out, and they are alive and well, what will you do then, Kirk?"

"Go back to my sutler's store at your camp. Hell, I'm making money, not rich money, but enough. And I know no savages are going to swoop down on me and lift my scalp. Yeah, I know official I ain't a sutler any more. Got an official franchise and we got a permanent store to sell to either civilians or soldiers. But I still like the name sutler."

A knock sounded on the door pole and someone jerked open the flap and stepped inside. Lt. Windsong snapped what started out to be salute that ended somewhere around his nose.

"Pickets all posted, sir!" There was no snap to the words. Halfway across the tent Kirk could smell the whiskey.

"Christ!" Captain Landower said. He jumped from his chair and his right fist crashed into the officer's jaw, dropping him to the floor.

"Christ, what a fucked-up mess! Help me get him back to his tent. I don't want the men to see him this way!"

"Probably too late for that, Captain," the scout said. "Probably about a half hour too damn late."

15

CHAPTER TWO

NIGHT WIRE
TO SPUR MCCOY
DENVER WILLOUGHBY HOTEL
DENVER COLORADO

PROCEED WITH ALL DUE SPEED TO OGDEN UTAH BY
RAIL. LOCATE HOSTILE UTE INDIAN TRIBE UNDER
CHIEF SPOTTED TAIL. NEGOTIATE OR WITH USE OF
FORCE, REMOVE FOUR WHITE GIRL CAPTIVES. ONE OF
PRIME IMPORTANCE, MISS PRISCILLA PATTERSON.
MISS PATTERSON IS NIECE OF SENATOR PATTERSON
OF MASSACHUSETTS WHO SITS ON THE COMMITTEE
THAT FUNDS, ADVISES, CONTROLS OUR OPERATION.
PRISCILLA'S RESCUE IMPERATIVE. REPORT SUCCESS
ONLY. TOP PRIORITY ASSIGNMENT. CONFIRM.

SIGNED WILLIAM WOOD, PRESIDENT CAPITOL IN-
VESTIGATIONS, WASHINGTON, D.C.

SPUR MCCOY HAD settled in for his train ride and
wished that the trip was over. He checked his
pocket watch. It was near dinner time and he
went to the dining car for a midday meal. He
never liked to eat much when he was loafing

this way, but just being conscious took some fuel for the body machine to work.

The diner was crowded and he was taken to a table for two that was already half occupied. The lady looked up quickly, smiled at Spur and nodded at the steward.

"Yes, Charles, you warned me I might be having company. It's perfectly all right."

She spoke with such assurance and self confidence that Spur was surprised and intrigued. Most women traveling alone were quiet, defensive and more than a little awed and frightened. This lady was just the opposite. She looked him squarely in the eye when he sat down, and held out her delicately formed hand with long fingernails that had been coddled, tended and, he thought, painted with a neutral shade of something.

"My name is Candice, I'm a poet and I'm going to San Francisco to visit my aunt." She looked at him expectantly.

"Good afternoon Miss Candice. I'm Spur McCoy and I'm going to Ogden."

"Oh, what a shame." She smiled. "Ogden is a nice little town, but stuffy hot and dry and San Francisco is so much more fun. What work do you do?"

"Investments," Spur said, then wished he had used something else. She obviously had money, from the looks of the two diamond rings on her right hand and the diamond decorated brooch at her throat. She wore an attractive brown day dress with a little matching jacket. It was an expensive outfit. Black, shining hair curled around her shoulders and framed her pretty face.

"You are in investments. Really. My father does that."

He ordered and she went back to her lunch. When the steward left with his order, he watched her. At last she laughed softly.

"Do you approve? You've been looking at me as if I were some kind of prize race horse on the auction block."

"Oh, sorry, it's a bad habit of mine. Whenever I see a beautiful woman I simply stare." He thought she would blush or lower her eyes or turn shy. She did none of those. Instead her chin came up a little and a spark glinted in her dark brown eyes.

"Don't be patronizing. I hate that. I'm supposed to dissolve into shyness and blush perhaps hide my face behind a napkin or fan. I hate those ideas. Thank you for saying I'm pretty. I can enjoy that without turning to mush."

The color rose in her cheeks as she spoke softly to him and he knew it was her show of anger at the system. Her words had the ring of fire and he knew he had touched a sensitive topic. Then her frown turned to a smile.

"Besides, I think you're the most handsome man I've seen on the train all day." She grinned delightedly and chuckled. "Do you know that I bribed Charley to bring you to my table? I've been waiting for you for almost an hour. First I

18

had ice water, and then coffee. At last I ordered, and now you're here."

Spur felt a touch of perspiration dampen his forehead. Now he was embarrassed. He grinned as he thought through what she had said. Few women these days were so outspoken. And she had waited for him to come.

"Candice, now I'm the one who's chagrinned. I'm pleased, but also curious as hell. Pardon my language. I'm curious. Do you always act so bold? Isn't it dangerous for a beautiful woman like you especially when traveling alone?"

She smiled. "Not unless I let it become dangerous. I like to think that instead it becomes exciting and unusual and fascinating. Our person to person relationships turn out to be just as pleasant or unhappy as we make them."

"Fine, a philosopher."

"Every person is a bit of a philosopher."

"True."

"You have to stop at Ogden?"

"Yes, I must."

"Oh." The one small word carried a world of disappointment. "Well, it is a nice little town, and it won't be too hot I'm sure."

"You said, Candice, that you're a poet?"

"Yes, Mr. McCoy, and Candice is my pen name and the only one that I use now."

"You sell your poetry?"

"Of course. You can't say you're a poet until you sell. I have four books of poems out, and another one almost finished. You'll be in one of my poems soon, I'm sure."

"That is interesting, and I'm flattered."

"You might not be, wait until you read the poem." She laughed. "Now I'm the one who's joking."

They finished their dinner and he helped hold her chair as she rose. It was the first time he could see how tall she was. He figured she was at least five feet seven inches, much taller than the average woman.

Outside the countryside was still high mountainous woodlands, consisting mostly of pine trees and a scattering of brilliantly colored aspens.

"May I see you to your seat?" Spur asked.

"If you don't I'll scream and scratch you," she said and grinned.

"Suffragette. You must be one of those."

"Of course, but their goals are just a beginning. I want total equality for men and women. A husband should not *own* his wife. She should have equal rights in property, voting, raising the children, in business and politics."

"Maybe, in a hundred years what you suggest would be possible. Not now, especially since only men make the nation's laws and hold all the offices. It might take a hundred and fifty years to achieve what you suggest."

"I'll wait," she said and they both laughed.

He guided her to her seat in the half-empty first class passenger car. It had plusher seats that were wider and more comfortable than in the coach section where Spur was riding.

"Sit down and let's talk. I'm curious about you," she said. He started to sit across from her, but she touched his arm and indicated a place beside her. As he sat down his leg brushed against hers and she smiled.

"Now, your accent. You must be from the East. I'd say New York."

"Right."

"But there's also a Northeast twang, maybe Maine for a few years, or Vermont?"

"I spent four years in Massachusetts."

"Yes, Harvard, how could I have missed that!"

"You're very good."

She smiled. "True."

The conductor came through. They would be stopping for Ogden passengers in fifteen minutes. Candice got up and walked after the trainman, caught him and spoke with him for a few moments, then came back. She smiled broadly.

"Now, what were we talking about?" She reached out and touched his arm and it sent a shock wave through him. "Now, I remember, Harvard. My brother went there. An ungrateful boy. Refused to go into the family business with father. Four generations our family has run the firm. Instead he stayed on at Harvard and took a masters degree and now he's studying for his doctorate in some special field of archeology."

"He wants to know how we got here."

"So it seems. Sure you don't want to go to San Francisco with me? We could see the sights and go to plays and concerts . . ."

"I'd love to, but duty calls."

"I've heard that often enough. How can I do a

good poem about you if I can't know you well enough?"

"How about calling it *Stranger on a Train*. Then you can get across that idea."

She trilled with laughter, reached over and kissed his cheek.

"Delightful! I am going to write a poem called that and use you in it. It's not often someone gives me an idea, a character and the title of a poem all at once."

They talked a while more, then he said he had to get ready to leave at Ogden. She took his hand as they said goodbye.

"Perhaps we'll run into each other again. I bet you're staying at the Harbour House Hotel in Ogden."

He shook his head. "No, the Ogden Railway Hotel. It's convenient."

They smiled once more, and he left. She was the most interesting woman he had met in years. She had a mind of her own, she was positive and forward looking, and he guessed that she would be a real fighter for women's equality.

Then the train began to slow and he hurried to his seat to pick up the notebook he had been using and to find a small carpetbag. When the train stopped, he stepped off hoping that his large carpetbag would be unloaded here as they promised.

Ogden was not as large as he had expected. It had been founded in 1847 when the Mormons arrived in Utah, but it had not grown the way

Salt Lake City had. The town was more dry and bleak than exciting.

Spur loosened his brown tie as he stood on the platform waiting for his baggage. There was a flurry at the baggage car and two porters rushed up with a wheeled cart and began taking off suitcases and carpetbags and two steamer trunks. He walked in that direction hoping his bag might be among them.

He stood watching the unloading when a porter looked past him.

"You said twelve, Miss Candice. That's zactly what we got, where can I take them for you?"

Spur turned around and saw Candice who now wore a soft blue blouse that seemed to emphasize her flat chest.

"Willy, thank you, you're so thoughtful. You can take them to the Railway Hotel. Oh, Mr. McCoy is going there too. Why don't you find his bags and take them all at one time?"

She linked her arm through his and pulled herself against him until he felt the warmth of her side.

"Hello, Miss Candice. Fancy meeting you here like this. Looks like a nice wayside stop on your way to San Francisco."

Candice smiled and hugged his arm.

"My schedule is flexible, I hope yours is too." She looked up at him with her softening brown eyes, and Spur smiled.

"My schedule is remarkably flexible."

Twenty minutes later they had registered in the hotel, asked for rooms on the same floor and

Spur had washed up and changed into a less formal sporting jacket and clean shirt. It was just after one in the afternoon. He checked his appearance in the wavy mirror over the dresser, went out his door and knocked two doors down on 314.

No one answered. He knocked again.

The door opened and Candice looked out. She wore the same blouse, but her dark hair was freshly brushed, her face scrubbed and a touch of red showed on cheeks and lips.

"May I come in?"

"Oh, goodness no, our chaperon isn't here," Candice laughed and opened the door. The room was like his, small, with a bed and two chairs and dresser and the same wavy mirror.

She walked away from him.

"Mr. McCoy, I don't want you to think I'm an easy woman. Just because I travel by myself, and enjoy talking to handsome men on a train, does not mean I have low moral standards."

"Of course not, Miss Candice."

"Just because I think you're a terrifically handsome man with a lean, trim marvelous body, does not mean that you can march in here and . . . and have your way with me."

"I understand that, Candice."

She walked back to him, reached up and kissed his lips, holding on to his jacket with both hands.

"Just because I enjoy kissing interesting, exciting men like you does not mean that I'm going to tear off my clothes for you and jump naked on the bed."

His arms came around her and he pulled her roughly against him, then bent and kissed her again and she flowed toward him, touching every part of her body against him that she could until the kiss ended.

She moaned softly, and looked up at him. "So nice! You seem to know just what I need."

He reached down and caught her legs and picked her up. She yelped and put her arms around his neck. Then she kissed him. Her tongue brushed his lips and they opened and she murmured deep in her throat as she pushed her delicate tongue into his mouth.

Holding the kiss, he carried her to the bed and sat down with her on his lap. The kiss went on and on and slowly he bent backward on the bed, lying down, drawing her firmly on top of him.

She purred and her tongue drove into his mouth searching for his. He could feel her body heat building and building. The searing hotness of her thighs burned through the fabric of her skirt and roasted him.

She broke off the kiss and pushed up. She leaned on one hand and patted her chest. "Yes, that is marvelous, and I'm just sorry I don't have big tits for you to play with. A woman should have big cow teats for you, but I just don't. Most women who are slender don't have big tops. But me . . . damn, if I'd been a Jersey milk cow, they would have shot me for supper!"

"You don't hear me complaining, do you Candice?" He pulled her face down to him and kissed her again, then sat up and pecked another kiss on her lips.

"Now, go ahead, seduce me," he said.

She frowned.

"You don't expect with all that women's equality and suffragette talk that I'm going to be the dominant one."

She laughed softly, and pulled off his jacket, then undid his tie and worked on his shirt buttons.

"Yes, I like this!" she said, her brown eyes glinting with sparks of victory and sexual excitement. When she had his shirt off she ran her hands over the hair on his chest, fondled his small nipples and kissed them.

"Yours are almost as big as mine." Then she grinned and pushed him down and lay on him again, kissing him and humping her hips at him. She was up a minute later unbuttoning his fly, then opening his belt and starting to pull off his pants.

"Oops! Boots first." She turned, and sat on his legs and then stood with her back to him and pulled off his boots one at a time. She forgot about his stockings and went back to his pants.

"My God! You've got a strange swelling down there," she said. "We're going to have to do something to reduce this terrible problem."

"Think of something," Spur said laughing.

She pulled his pants off and the short underwear, then his socks. When he was naked she stood there looking at him.

"My God! but the human male is a beautiful animal! There is nothing like him in the universe! So trim, so wonderfully proportioned.

I wish I were a damn artist so I could paint you nude."

Spur lay there a moment longer, then sat up. "Your turn," he said.

She stepped back. "I'm the dominant one, I get to take off my own clothes." She did, making a tease as she stripped out of her garments one at a time.

"You don't know that I can dance, do you?" She ground her hips at him and pulled back, did a series of quick little turns and spun out of her blouse, then threw a thin chemise away and stood for him to look. Her breasts were small, like a thirteen-year-old's. He stood and kissed them, then sat down as she continued her dance. When she had taken off her skirt and the three petticoats she wore only silk drawers. They bound at her waist and extended down each leg to her knee. They were fancy, with blue bows and lace. Slowly she pulled them down, showing the fringes of pubic hair, then farther and farther until they fell to her feet.

Spur stood and picked her up in his arms and carried her to the bed and placed her on the fancy quilted comforter, then kissed her gently on the lips and lay down beside her.

"No more games?" Spur asked.

"Oh, God, no! No more games, just love me!"

With his hands he began a gentle seduction, warming her small breasts, working down her torso, kissing her lips, her face, her throat until she was writhing with desire.

"Now, darling, push him in me now. I need him!"

Spur worked down lower, teasing around her crotch, lightly touching her wet nether lips, then drifting away.

"Damnit, Spur. Fuck me right now before I explode!"

He went over her, found the opening and slid into her as she yelled and squealed in excited relief and passion.

Before he was fully inserted she climaxed.

Candice believed in showing her emotions, and now she screeched out her ecstasy as her climax rolled on and on. He held his hand over her mouth to quiet the sound, her eyes widened and she nodded, then climaxed again.

Her legs lifted around his torso and ankles locked together, lifting her hips slightly off the bed. Spur began probing and thrusting with the rhythm of a drum building from slower to faster and with longer and longer strokes.

Candice climaxed twice more and each time she let everyone on the hotel floor know it. When Spur came to his eruption she joined him in yet another fulfillment and they humped and pounded and clawed and snarled at each other.

When it was over she pushed away from him at once and curled into a fetal ball on the far side of the bed. At first he thought she was crying, then he saw she was not. After ten minutes he touched her shoulder but she pulled away.

"I need to be alone for a few minutes," she said.

He turned back and drifted off into a nap. When he came awake she was still naked and sitting crosslegged close to him. She held a .32 caliber pistol in her hand and the muzzle pressed against the side of his head. She watched him with a curious expression.

Spur looked up at her without moving. The weapon was at the right angle so he could see a deadly lead slug in one of the cylinders. They all had to be full.

"Candice."

"Don't talk, just lie there. I need to think. I can tell you all about it because you're a good listener. I write, but to write you must experience. Look how Bret Hart and Mark Twain go running around the country. They couldn't write half of what they do if they didn't *experience* those things. That's why I travel, and meet kind strangers, like you."

She looked up at his eyes, taking her glance away from the muzzle of the pistol where it touched his head.

"I was wondering . . . just wondering, what it would feel like to actually kill someone. I mean to *know* that I had taken another life. How would I react? What would I be thinking about? What would the emotions be inside me as I pulled the trigger, and I saw Spur's head jolt sideways with the sudden impact of the bullet, then the blood and the sound of it, the splatter of the blood, the look on your face and finally your breath stopping and maybe your bladder emptying? What would my reaction be to knowing that you were dead, and I did it? How in hell would I feel?"

"I can tell you," Spur said.

"You?"

"Yes, it wouldn't exactly be the same, but I could tell you how I felt when I killed for the first time."

"You've killed more than once? Men all, or any women?"

"Women too."

"Oh, God! Tell me."

She took the pistol away from his head, lay it out of reach on a small stand, then leaned back and kissed his head where the metal had touched him.

She lay beside him, touching him, then took his hand and pushed it between her spread legs. She reached over and held his limp phallus.

"Now, Spur McCoy. Tell me what it feels like to kill for the very first time."

He did.

She listened, she fantasized, she vicariously experienced the killing, and she understood.

CHAPTER THREE

HIS FIRST EVENING in Ogden, Spur McCoy went to the address he had been supplied by Washington. He arrived at the appointed time, seven P.M. All he knew was that he was supposed to meet a local man, Ezekiel Smith, a Mormon, one of the officials in the Ogden church. Smith was supposed to know something about the Utes, how they functioned, where they gathered, where they might be now.

When he found the house after asking four different people where it was, he saw that it was like most of the others, built of sturdy red brick. Brick is warm in the winter and cooler in the summer, and the Mormons owned the brickyard.

He knocked and a man two inches shorter than Spur's own six foot two inches opened the door.

"Mr. Ezekiel Smith?" Spur asked.

It elicited a cautious yes from the wide-bodied man.

"My name is Spur McCoy, I was told to contact you here about information regarding the Ute Indians. I understand you're the local expert on the habits of the redmen."

Smith stood where he was, barring his home from this outsider. Slowly he shook his head.

"Ain't an expert no more, Mr. McCoy. One time I did know them Utes inside out. Fact is I did some early trapping and supply hunting up in the mountains where they was. Got along fine with them, nobody got riled, or shot up anybody else. And I never overtrapped on any of my lines. Years back. Can't help you now."

Someone evidently spoke to Smith whom Spur couldn't see. At last he stepped back.

"But come in, we'll talk. Not much I can help you with about where they are now. It was twenty years ago that I was up in the hills."

Spur stepped inside the neat house. It was as if the place was ready for a general's inspection. Spotless, well furnished in plain, no-nonsense wooden fashion with homemade cushions and pillows. A braided rug lay on the wooden floor. The big fireplace was cold but racks and hooks were in place where one fire could both heat and cook food. Economical, thrifty.

A small woman in a plain gray dress stood to the side. Her hair was still long, but she was in her forties, and looked worn out. When she smiled her face lit up remarkably.

"Could I get you a cold glass of lemonade, Mr. McCoy? We just made a fresh pitcher."

Smith waved her away. "Yes, yes, bring two glasses and the pitcher." Smith went to one of the chairs and motioned Spur to sit in the other one.

"The Wastch mountains. Not as high as some, but keep you puffing to climb them. That's where the Utes live. They used to make raids all around. See, the Utes are hunters and raiders. The army calls them warlike. Not so. They don't go to war, they jab at you, and raid, and jab, and raid and eventually the outlying settlers moved out before they lost all their livestock, and then their daughters. Utes do love to bring back girls from raids on other tribes as well as whites."

"I understand there are two Mormon girls in the Spotted Tail camp right now, Mr. Smith."

The Mormon looked at him sternly. "A white woman captured by the Utes is as good as dead. She won't last more than three or four months, depending how easy the squaws are on her. It's the squaws who beat and torment the captives, send them wild and crazy before long. Then sometimes the squaws go too far and kill the girl captives."

"Have you had any luck rescuing the two Mormon girls?"

Smith shook his head. "No. We have not tried. Once a girl is taken and subjected to the Indian men and the Indian ways, she is not able to return to our society and live a normal life. She is lost, her physical body is lost. We concentrate on saving her soul."

The small woman came back with two glasses, and behind her walked a woman in her twenties. She was pretty, her hair combed carefully, her dress plain but with touches to make it more attractive. She was slender with a fine figure. The younger woman carried the pitcher.

33

He motioned them away after they put down the drinks on the small table.

The younger woman frowned.

"Ezekiel, it is terribly impolite not to introduce people."

He sighed, pointed at the woman who spoke. "Mr. McCoy, this here is Ruth, and her mouth is going to get her turned into a pillar of salt one of these days." Ruth grinned and nodded shyly now that she had goaded the man. "Ruth is my wife." He paused and turned to the older woman. "This is Esther, my first wife." He paused a moment and looked up. Spur nodded to both women.

"I'm pleased to meet you both, the lemonade looks delicious."

They smiled and left the room.

When Spur looked up at the Mormon polygamist again, his face was as neutral as he could make it.

"Where do the Utes usually move to for their winter quarters?" Spur asked.

Smith seemed relieved that he was not questioned about his multiple marriages. He poured the lemonade and Spur saw ice floating in it.

"Usually they went to the two-forks area. That's a river well up in the mountains, probably fifty miles from here. It's low enough in a valley to protect them from the hardest snow storms."

Spur took out a map from his light blue jacket pocket and unfolded it. It showed Ogden at the very edge, and then extended eastward and northward showing the Wastch mountains all the way to the Idaho border. The mountain range ran north and south.

"We used to call the place Round Valley. Don't know what they call it now. It's north past Logan and off toward Bear Lake."

"But, like you say, it's been twenty years. Mr. Smith, do you know of any of the other men around here who have had any dealings with the Utes? Men who might know where to find them, right now?"

He took a long drink of the lemonade, then shook his head.

"Not so I could think of one. The Utes pulled back from our people. We trained all our outlying setters to shoot and use a knife. When the Utes came up on the losing end of two or three raids in a row, old Spotted Tail decided he wanted easier prey."

"My only other question is about renegades, town Indians. Any of them around I might hire to act as guides to get back into the mountains and find the winter camp?"

"Was one. Everybody called him Injun. But he drank himself to death a year ago. Nobody knew where he got the whiskey."

"Nobody else?"

Before Smith could answer Spur heard a chatter of young voices and twelve children from three to ten thundered into the room. They all needed a goodnight kiss. Smith hugged each one, whispered something into eager ears, and then kissed them and sent them along. The youngest came first, then the older ones. All wore identical white muslin nightgowns, easy to make, easy to wash, inexpensive, and only two sizes so interchangeable.

When the last child was gone, Smith turned back.

"Mr. McCoy, that's my total fund of facts about the Utes. I don't know of any other town Indian Utes we have. Now, anything else?" He stood, indicating to Spur that the talk was over.

It was. Spur walked toward the door. Not much help. He reached out his hand.

"Thank the ladies for the lemonade, and thank you for your talk about the Utes. I'll find somebody who knows the country."

Smith opened the door, shook his hand and Spur went outside. The door closed quickly behind him.

On his way back to the hotel, Spur did not see the small person who followed him. She had coal black hair, worn long, a small round face with blue eyes, and a snub nose. At first glance people thought she was Indian, then when they saw her blue eyes they wondered about Mexican Indian, or perhaps Spanish.

Those who knew her called her Istas, an Indian name meaning snow. But long ago she had learned that she did not belong with the round eyes, and the Indians had abandoned her to freeze in a snowbank when she was only two years old. A trapper had found her and raised her as one of his own children—until she began to look so much like an Indian. Now Ezekiel Smith would not even talk to her.

Istas trudged along, well in back of the white man, knowing that she must find out where he stayed. Perhaps since he was searching for the Ute tribe, she could help him. Perhaps. In this world of Mormons she had learned well that it might have been better for her to have perished in the snow the way the Utes had intended. But somewhere deep within her a voice cried out against that idea.

She was *somebody*. Somewhere there was a better life for her. She was *important*. Someday she would find her place.

Ahead she saw the white man go into the Railway Hotel. She had a friend who worked there. He would help her. For now she must go back to her hut behind the stables. They let her live there if she cleaned the stables every day. If one of the customers at the stable was kind enough to give her a nickel or a dime, she could eat. Otherwise she often went for two or three days without eating.

Then she relied on her Indian instincts and stole. It was not wrong to steal to eat. That was basic survival. She came to the stable, slipped in the far door and stretched out on the three horse blankets that had been left in the stalls. She felt close to them, they were like her, abandoned, helpless, alone. She curled up and went to sleep. Tonight she had eaten. Now and then the nice lady, Ruth, sent word she should come to the back door for a hearty meal. Ruth was the nicest lady in the whole world.

CHAPTER FOUR

YATES LEANED ON the shovel and puffed. He surveyed the fruits of his sweat for the past three weeks and decided it had been worth it. The sluice was a foot wide and nearly twenty feet long. They had raised the baffles to an inch high. They were nailed to the bottom of the sluice to catch the gold.

It had worked before, it would work this time, even though this Utah country was contrary, mean, arid and downright nasty. They had at last found a favorable looking dig near enough to a small stream. Finding enough running water in that part of Utah to establish a workable flume and sluice panning operation was as hard as finding an honest man in a gold rush town.

Twenty feet up the hill near the head of the sluice box, the second man in the gold panning team stood up from the pit where he had been digging. His name was Barlow and he was a larger man, a foot taller than Yates, stooped with his sixty years of chasing gold, but still with an iron will and his thin blood sprinkled liberally with gold dust.

Barlow had hit it big in the Forty-Niner rush out in California, lost it all in a crooked business deal and since then had been working the various strikes from Virginia City to Mexico. He'd often talked about trying the Black hills of South Dakota. There had been gold stories about the Black Hills for years.

"Damn, we got her, Barlow," Yates said, stretching his back. "You want to open the sluice gate up there?"

"No lie, Yates? You said it wouldn't be done until tomorrow."

"Done by damn, take a look if you think I'm lying."

"Take it easy, Yates. I believe you." He used the shovel as a crutch to get on the first step he had cut into the small pit, then rolled over the top of the hole.

The tiny stream was no more than two feet wide and two inches deep. But they decided there was enough water to do the job. The sluice went straight down the course of the stream, so they could reuse the water lower down if they hit any good looking gravel.

"Open her up by damn!" Yates shouted.

Barlow put his hand on the inch-think board a foot wide that kept the flow of the stream out of the sluice. Then he looked at Yates and prayed silently that this would be a strike, just a little bit of color to encourage them. Yates especially needed some color.

"Here she goes!" Barlow shouted and pulled up the board. Six inches of built-up water rushed into the twenty foot long wooden flume, washing ahead of it the inch deep covering of sand, gravel and they hoped gold dust, flakes and even a nugget or two.

The surge of water slowed, then more water came and within a minute or two muddy water poured from the end of the flume back into the creek.

"By damn, she works!" Yates screeched. He sidestepped along the wooden trough watching the water working the gravel, pushing the lighter stones and silt over the baffles, washing the worthless part downstream. Yates knew it would be some time before they discovered if they had any dust.

He sat down beside the flume he had worked on so hard and closed his eyes and looked up at the sky. Damn but it hurt these days. Why did a man have to turn sixty-five? He found more parts of him that ached every day.

Barlow was beside him almost at once.

"Hey, Yates, you all right? Look a little red in the face."

"I'm fine. Just wanted to sit a minute." He touched the flume. "We did it again, Barlow you old desert rat! Got us a real placer outfit again!" He reached up and brushed wetness from his eyes. "Damned if she ain't working!"

"Course she's working. Think we should celebrate. Let me get that jug." Barlow walked up the hill to a camp, and came back with a pint whiskey bottle. He looked at the water running over the sand and gravel and nodded.

"Washing that gravel like old Harley Ned! We'll know tonight if we got anything good going here." He gave the bottle to Yates who unscrewed the top and took a shot. He lifted the bottle.

"Here's to the next big strike!" Yates drank again and passed the bottle.

"Yeah, even a little strike. We need some color, Yates." He drank.

Yates reached for the pint. "Hey, Barlow, ever think we'd end up this way, slaving on some God forsaken side of a mountain, pissing on a flat rock and wishing we had a good woman?"

"Nobody thinks about ending any way but rich. Least not placer men like us." He grinned. "Woman? Hell, Yates, you've forgot what to do with a woman, good or bad."

"Hell I have! Try me out with one of them twenty year old city girls sometime."

"Next time we hit a whorehouse your treat is on me, but you got to tell me if you can still make it."

"Hell of a fat chance of me collecting."

Barlow stood and checked the sluice. "Ain't like we had a full fledged river charging through this box. We got to help some with the bigger rocks. But the sand will wash just fine. Come supper time we can check them first few baffles."

Yates slumped against the rocks. "Hell, tell the butler to have the upstairs maid take off her blouse and get down here."

"Senile, the old coot done finally gone senile," Barlow said.

"Just dreaming a little bit. You seen any

damn Indians around here? This is Ute country. Hey, I could even go for one of them little Ute girls."

"Damn, he really is senile," Barlow snorted. "Just so he does his half of the work."

"Wonder if them Utes still got them four white girls they captured off the train, spell back?" Yates asked.

"Probably. Nobody with a whit of sense would go after them, not in the Ute's own territory."

"Somebody will. Army, probably. Y'know I was in the army for one enlistment."

"Yeah?" Barlow asked.

"Long time ago. Before the war. Never shot nobody."

Barlow went to the head of the sluice box and put his hands in the water.

"Come look at this, Yates. Coming along fine!"

When Yates came they checked the first three baffles. There were a few large rocks which they examined and threw out. Along the back of the second inch-high baffle lay a thin golden sheen.

"A trace, Yates! We've got some color! Next few baffles down should be enough to scrape off. Goddamn, real gold dust! Yahoooooooo!"

Yates touched the gold sheen, tried to rub some off on his finger. Most of it washed off by the time his finger came out of the water. But there was a touch left. He looked at it, then tears came and he cried and touched the gold and sat down beside the box and tried to wipe away the tears. They were old man tears and he hated them.

"Barlow, you screeching windbag. If this is a dream, you sure as hell better not wake me up. If this is a dream I'll kick your ass over half the county."

Barlow had been working down the sluiceway, throwing out larger rocks. He found the board that had had acted as a gate on the sluice and put it in again, stopping the water. When a small pond had built up behind the gate in the tiny stream, he opened the gate and let the water surge down again.

"It's working. What we need now is a larger pool of water upstream. We got to dig a pond, then let the water through all at once, a kind of flood to make the sluicing work better."

"Hell, I ain't no damn ditchdigger."

"You are now. We need more water volume to work more sand. And there is gold here, you old coot! More water, more sand and more fucking gold!"

Yates sat up, stood slowly and picked up a pointed shovel.

"You said the magic word, Barlow. But when we're rich and famous and sitting at a big party on nob hill in San Francisco, I ain't gonna let you push me around this way."

Barlow shot a squirt of tobacco juice at Yates but missed. Then they began deciding where to dig the pool and how to keep the whole thing higher than the opening of the sluice so they would have a gravity fall on the water.

Yates slammed his shovel into the ground.

"Hate digging ditches," Yates said, then he grinned thinking about the gold.

Lt. Joseph Windsong sat in his tent and stared through the open flap at the wooded downslope. He had his field quarters positioned so he could not see the troops, only the peaceful woods. He wanted to hear the chatter of the nearby stream.

He had his orderly launder the clothes he wore during the Ute attack. He couldn't bear to think of what had happened.

It was his first time in battle! Yes and he had come through with his colors in the mud, in the shit was a better description. His father would kill him. No quarter, his damn general father would throw him out of the army so fast he would think he was going over Niagra Falls.

Windsong stood and paced. He wanted to please his father. All his life he had been trying to please his strict disciplinarian father. He had been doing it for so long, during military lower grade schools, and prep military school and at last West Point, where he had squeaked through.

What the hell now?

He stared at the peaceful countryside.

What in the name of God was he going to do?

He could always get killed in battle and make his father deliriously happy. But that had some drawbacks.

Lt. Windsong decided he must lead the next fight, push his men into Ute territory and gain a great victory.

He could rescue the white girl, the damn senator's niece, and be a real hero. He would volunteer for the party to go into the Ute camp and bring out the girl. If Captain Landower refused him the chance, he would lead a party of volunteers himself, by damn!

The infantry officer stood and walked around his tent. He had to get the old swagger back. The old bravado he had developed when he was at the Point and lording it over the underclassmen. The military style. Goddamnit he was an officer! He would redeem himself in the eyes of the captain and the men. He knew they were laughing at him. They wouldn't laugh when he came back with Spotted Tail's head on a guideon, and all four of the white girls!

Yes, he could do it . . . he would do it!

Lt. Windsong marched out of his tent and up the little creek to the commander's tent. He would get this started right now. He went into the captain's tent after knocking and hearing the word to enter. He had rinsed his head in the stream earlier, and all traces of the drink were gone. The sudden drinking had been a foolish, immature act. He was confident now, sure of himself.

Outside it was almost dark. He stood at attention before the captain's desk and saluted when his superior looked up.

"Sir, I was at fault today, and totally wrong. I wish to right this wrong. I wish to volunteer to lead the raid on Spotted Tail's camp and rescue the white girls. I'll advise you of the size force I need when we discover his lair and I've had a chance to evaluate his defenses and work out my own plan of attack."

Captain Landower looked up from the map he had been studying.

"Windsong, there might not even be an attack. We hope to parley. If that's impossible, stealth, not a cavalry charge, will probably stand a better chance of success."

Lt. Windsong started to interrupt but Landower hurried on.

"Your offer has been noted. It may be some days before we even find the hostiles, let alone prepare for any battle. Until that time I would suggest that you perform your duties with outstanding military snap and polish, that you try to regain some of your lost dignity and control over your troops. Right now I wouldn't let you lead a slit trench detail outside our walking guards. You're excused, Lieutenant!"

Lt. Windsong felt his face burning as he saluted smartly, did a formal about face and marched out of the tent. He went at once to the sergeant of the guard and inspected the posts, the men and the walking routes. He changed two of them. He sent a rider to check on the four outlying pickets, then he sent for Sergeant Bennedict to report to his quarters.

Sgt. Bennedict knocked on the officer's door and stepped inside. He was not in full uniform.

Lt. Windsong chewed him out for five minutes about his lack of respect for an officer by appearing out of uniform. Then the talk took a new direction.

"Sergeant, you are aware that you assaulted

me today, in direct violation of military discipline."

"Lt. Windsong, I saved your life. If you had taken a dozen more steps you would have been shot so full . . ."

The enlisted man stopped. He could feel the hatred boiling from the officer.

"Sergeant, you are aware that you usurped my authority, you assumed my command, you evidently reported all of this over my head to my commanding officer. If we were in garrison duty you would be reduced to the rank of private, courtmartialed, and probably be made to serve from fifteen to twenty years in a federal prison."

"You got two troopers killed this morning, Sir. You made the mistake of riding into the trap. In garrison duty few troopers are killed because of the stupidity of their officers."

"You insubordinate . . ."

"How are you going to prove I said that? Lieutenant, you've been in the army for three years. I've been in almost twenty. I can out-soldier you in any category or job you want to pick. I'll go one on one against you with knives, pistols or bare fists. You just take those bars off and we'll find a nice private place out in the woods right by damn now!"

Sergeant Bennedict tightened his hands into big fists, and stood, feet wide, his face as red as a cloudy sunset, and his eyes glaring hard at the man he hated with all his soul.

"You would like that, wouldn't you, Sergeant? Forget it, it's not going to happen.

Instead you're going to help me win back my respect in this outfit. You'll be hearing from me shortly, now you're dismissed!''

The sergeant glared at Lt. Windsong, but snapped him a salute that was not returned, and stormed silently out of the tent.

Lt. Windsong's plan was forming. It would of necessity be a surprise stroke, a dashing, daring raid that would leave the hostiles in disarray and their captives freed. Sergeant Bennedict would play an important part in the mission, a most important part. So important that he might die for the cause.

Lt. Windsong sat in the folding chair carried by the supply and mess wagon and smiled. He would show them all! He would set the record straight once and for all. He was a Windsong, damnit! One of these days he would have a general's stars on his shoulders, but not quite yet.

First he had to take care of this small problem that had come up today with the damnable Ute savages. They would pay for their part in his temporary dishonor as well. But mostly Sergeant Bennedict would pay. The trooper had manhandled him, and in front of the other enlisted men. Such an affront could not be allowed to go unpunished.

It wouldn't. And that day of reckoning would come soon!

CHAPTER FIVE

CHIEF SPOTTED TAIL sat cross-legged near a small fire in front of his tepee in the northern reaches of the Wastch mountains. He was in a new winter camp where he could see for several miles down a long valley. It was said the winter would not be so harsh here, and the summers sweet because of plenty of water.

Spotted Tail also selected the area because it would be easy to defend. To the back of the camp of some thirty tepees and hogan-like thatched and wooden poled dwellings, a cliff rose more than a hundred feet. In front of the camp a small river ran past, and on both sides the pine trees flourished, giving them shelter as well as plenty of fuel for their fires.

The chief stared into the fire, trying to find some kind of a sign, some omen that the Great Spirit was with him, that all would be well. He found no sign.

He looked up as his white squaw came to the door of the tepee and motioned that she had his evening meal ready. He watched her with delight. Never before had he bought a captive from one of his braves, but this blonde, big breasted round eyed girl fascinated him as no woman ever had.

Perhaps he spent too much time studying the ways of the round eyes. He knew that the Pony Soldiers were coming. He had seen several skirmishes with them, fought in one, and knew that the Pony Soldiers would eventually win every battle until there were no more Indian warriors of *any nation!*

He had been told there were a million white men under arms, warriors who could use the long rifles well. To Spotted Tail a million was an unending supply. He didn't know the white man's ways with figures, but he knew there were a million stars, and a million grains of sand on the shore of a large river. A million was more round eye rifles than all the Indians in the mountains and plains could hope to defeat.

He groaned as he rose and went inside his tepee. The white squaw was there. She continually brought him his food on a tin plate he had stolen on a raid. Spotted Tail admitted that she was a good cook, and fixed food better and in many more ways than his other squaw had.

He touched her golden hair that fell almost to her waist, stroking it. She turned and smiled.

"My, but you must be feeling gentle today. You've been thinking again about your people."

Spotted Tail stared at her, wishing he knew what her words meant. He shrugged and reached out and fondled her swaying white breasts. He made her remain in the tepee most of the time so she would stay white. He had noticed that her skin turned bright red the first few days on the trail back from the hated railway. He put a stolen jacket around her and kept her shaded.

Now he made her wear only the skirt he had captured her in, so he could watch her beautiful swaying, full, pointed breasts. She was his treasure, a stolen treasure, true, but a bright spot in his mountains of woes.

He knew the Pony Soldiers would be coming after the captives, given time. That was one reason he had moved his winter camp here. His other two squaws were working on his winter house. It would be made of logs set on end side by side into the ground to form a square. Mud plaster would chink the slits between the logs. More logs would form a flat roof six feet off the ground. A foot of dirt would be thrown on the roof, then sod dug up and planted there to insure a waterproof ceiling.

"You can let go of me now and eat your supper. Eat," she said, making eating motions.

The chief nodded, a touch of a smile on his face. She was a constant delight to him. Before he had thought of squaws as little more than possessions. True they relieved his loins, and in his youth he had a touch of affection for Walking Bird, but now she was old and ugly.

A sudden urge to lay on his pallet with this white one and do the many strange things she needed him to do to her to make her satisfied pulled at him. He reached for her legs, but she shook her head and pointed at his food and made shivering, cold motions.

Yes, he would eat his meat first while it was

51

warm. She made a strange white man's food she called bread, that he found more tasty than the pemmican he often ate. He had eaten many bird eggs, but ever since one raiding party had brought back a dozen chickens, his white squaw had taken them over and harvested the eggs they laid. She fed them to him in various ways. Strange.

He ate the roasted meat, venison from a fresh kill, and saw that it was not burned on the outside as most of the roasted meat he ate usually was. He would find out how she did it.

Spotted Tail knew that his other two squaws hated this blonde one. He had given her special privileges and she did not have to do the usual squaw work. When he found the women on the village taunting her he quietly ordered them to stop. Lashing them with his tongue he told them never to touch her again.

He did not lift a hand to help the other three white females captured in the raid. All were young, one yet not a woman. The young one was treated as a child by the brave who captured her. He vowed that she would be raised for another two or three years and then become his white squaw.

As the chief ate his meal with his fingers, Priscilla Patterson watched. She would eat after he did. It was simply the way things were here. She was smart enough to adapt to Indian ways, but she had also bent many of their rules and methods of doing things. The chief preferred her to cook for him, indicating the other squaws cooked food fit only for the camp dogs. She had been pleased.

She looked down at her breasts and realized it didn't bother her anymore to be undressed this way. At first it had, and she hid herself with her hands when outside. Now it seemed natural. Of course she had bigger breasts than anyone here, except the one Mormon girl, and that pleased her.

Priscilla shuddered, remembering that first night on the trail when Spotted Tail had raped her. She had fought him like a lioness, until he had hit her. Then she submitted, but the second and third time, she showed him a different way of satisfying the chief. She got the impression no woman had even taken him in her mouth before.

Right then she was glad she was not totally sexually inexperienced. She could thank her brother and her uncle for her early training. Her brother was three years older and they had played doctor and other little sexual games since she had begun to have breasts. It was a long time before he actually penetrated her vagina. He liked to be sucked off, and he told her that was less dangerous. For a long time she didn't know about getting pregnant, not until he told her.

She stretched now and went to the pallet. He would be ready in a moment. She sat on the hard mat she had become used to, then slid out of her skirt and let her knees drift apart as Spotted Tail watched.

He growled at her, threw down the piece of meat and came toward her.

In a tepee near the outer circle, Gertrude sat on her pallet and stared at Running Deer. She wore a dirty doeskin dress that was too small for her and barely covered her knees. Running Deer looked at her and she motioned him over, and lifted her skirt.

The brave laughed, said something she didn't understand and wagged his head at her. He held up three fingers, then touched his crotch and made a limp motion.

"Come on big brave, you can go one more time," Gertrude said, cupping her breasts and holding them up so they showed through the neck of the loose doeskin robe.

He chattered something at her and ducked out the tepee opening. A moment later two young braves came in with her husband/captor Ute behind them. Again he spoke. Gertrude refused to try to learn the lingo. The army would come rescue her soon enough. It was a waste of time.

The brave pushed both young men down on her pallet, then grabbed her garment and pulled it over her head. He left laughing as the two braves sat and stared. Then they fondled her and pulled off their own loin cloths and buckskin leggings.

Gertrude cackled with joy. She had never used two men at once. It mattered none that they were Indians. Soon she had one pumping between her legs and the other groaning as she pulled his erection into her mouth.

Nearer the chief's tent the fourth captive was held. She had a tightly tied long rawhide thong around one wrist and the other lashed to the back pole. She could move a dozen feet either way, but that was all. Twice she had run away. Twice she had been brought back and the squaws had beaten her back with switches until she bled. She wailed and cried and told them that she was a Mormon and would not let them violate her body.

Her captor was a small, squat brave who already had one squaw, and kept this white girl only until he could sell her for three horses. But none of the other braves wanted a squaw who would not willingly lay on her back and spread her legs. What else was a white squaw good for? She could not go into the woods and find berries or roots.

Once a day the short Indian known as Rutting Bear came to her and forced her to lay down and let him take her. Each time she fought, but as the days continued, she fought less and less. The brave nodded. She was much like a wild horse that needed to be broken. Soon she would be coming to him, asking him for sex.

Back in the chief's tent, a messenger came asking the chief to hear a complaint of one brave against another.

The chief and top members of the tribe assembled around the council fire. The important ceremonial area had been formed by deepening a shallow depression, until it was six feet below the outer rim some twenty feet from the center. A fire glowed as the sun began to go down. The charges were serious.

Flying Owl came and stood before the chief, and in low tones told how One Wrong Hand had caught Flying Owl's squaw while she was berry picking, had forced her into sex, and during the rape, he had accidentally killed her.

The story was not new, it had happened over a week ago, but Flying Owl first had to recover from his loss. More important he had to find out the facts to tell the chief. Now he had them all.

Chief Spotted Tail nodded as the story was told. He closed his eyes when it was over and looked at the heavens. There were no bad signs or omens. He looked at Flying Owl.

"Do as our customs demand," he said. The matter was closed. Then a rider reported to the council as a whole that he had come back from a long range game hunt and had found plenty of deer and wild fowl all the way to the end of the mountains to the north. Soon the council was over.

Flying Owl left the group and went to One Wrong Hand's tepee. The brave sat inside on his pallet, his two wives were seated on either side. He knew well the Ute laws. If a man killed a horse or a squaw belonging to another brave, and the chief approves, the injured man may then kill a like victim owned by the killer.

The squaws trembled as they touched One Wrong Hand. He looked at the older squaw and smiled. He had known her since he was a small boy. How could he harm her? He stared at the young squaw who had brought so much joy to One Wrong Hand.

He turned, said nothing and went through the tepee flap. Outside he walked straight to the picket area where the horses were tied. Some were penned into a makeshift corral. He found two horses belonging to One Wrong Hand, and swung his knife, cutting the throats of both horses. When he saw that they were dying, Flying Owl returned his knife to its sheath and went back to his lonesome tepee.

That night both squaws crept into One Wrong Hand's pallet. They would work together and make sure that he never had the need to take another man's wife by force. They would each make love to him twice a day, keeping him so worn out he would not even think of another brave's squaw.

Chief Spotted Tail sat in his lodge as his white squaw fed small sticks into the fire in the center of the tepee's fire ring. She had learned the techniques quickly; enough fuel to keep a small, bright fire going, but not one that would produce too much heat. The smoke and most of the heat rose straight upward and out the hole in the top of the tepee where the long aspen poles crossed.

He had seen the sign at the council fire, but had not told the others. The Blue Coats were coming. They would descend on the village like drops of rain in a thunderstorm and their rifle fire and swords would take a terrible toll. The meaning of the sign was clear. He had to send out sentries and scouts far into the hills along every trail that approached the valley.

He had to work out plans for a second winter camp where the tribe could move on a moment's notice. If the Pony Soldiers came toward this camp, they would find it deserted, and no trail left to follow.

It had to be done.

He stroked the white squaw's long blonde hair and used the comb she had brought with her. He combed her hair for a half hour but he barely heard or saw her, he was communing with the spirits again, trying to determine exactly the best course for the Ute Nation.

"We can't fight the Blue Coats," he said softly. "For they are like the fleas on a dog, without number . . . millions."

Priscilla looked at him, not understanding a word, but she knew he was a great chief of the Utes, and that he was concerned about his people.

Gently she took the comb from his hand, smoothed his brow, then brought one of his hands to her bare breasts, and slid the other hand under her red and white skirt. He blinked, frowned for a moment. Then he smiled and pushed her down on the pallet gently and continued communing with the spirits as she spread her legs and urged him into an erection.

CHAPTER SIX

WHEN SPUR McCoy returned to the Railway Hotel after he had talked with the local Mormon man, he dug into his carpetbag. First he emptied it on the bed, then pressed on one side of the bottom and a cleverly concealed secret compartment opened in the false bottom. He looked over papers there, and selected two. One proved who he was, the second authorized him by telegram to search out the Ute camp and rescue four captive white girls.

Twenty minutes later, Spur sat in the sheriff's private office and watched him read the papers. The lawman grunted.

Sheriff Gerald Derrick was the old West kind of law officer. Long on riding and shooting skills, and not as comfortable around paperwork and politicians. As in most Mormon towns he probably had been selected by church officials, asked to run and elected without any major opposition.

He was a medium sized man, but sturdy. Spur would have guessed he pounded iron in a blacksmith shop from the size of his arms and upper body.

"So somebody is going to try. We've got two girls from here in town up there someplace. I'm not going in them mountains."

"I can understand that, Sheriff Derrick. The Utes know every rock and trail and spring in a hundred square miles. They would cut a posse to pieces, and more than likely you would never see them."

"Damn true." He leaned back, his frown slowly dissolved, as he gained new respect for this government man. He handed back Spur's papers. Spur folded them and put them in his jacket pocket.

"So what are you going to do? I can help you as much as you need."

"Information, mostly. I'm looking for a town Ute, or somebody who knows those mountains as well as the Ute scouts do. Anybody around?"

"Month ago I was thinking the same way when we talked about going up there to get the girls back. Was a couple of town Injuns here, but one got himself killed in a knife fight and the other one took off into the woods. Never seen him again."

"Anybody else?"

The sheriff stood and walked to the window and looked out on his quiet town. Never much went wrong in a good Mormon town like this one. Not a saloon in town, no gambling, no fancy women. Not at all like some towns he had been a law man in.

"There is Robbie." He shook his head. "Sometimes he's worse than useless. But if you get about two beers in him and hold him there, he

60

can make sense. Did a lot of trapping back in the mountains. Hung on for years after everybody else got scared out. Said the Ute caught him once. He showed them he had only critters that they never hunted, fox and some beaver. They made a friend of him and he came and went as he wanted."

"Sounds like my man."

"Depends if he's on a two week drunk or not."

A hour later, Spur found Robbie just outside the city limits in a tavern-inn. He had been dumped outside near the stables, not because he was drunk, but because he had been bothering regular customers begging drinks.

Robbie was in his forties, well worn, with a face that looked like it had been eroded by the Colorado river. Bleary eyes peered up at Spur when he hunkered down beside him.

"Robbie, I've got a job for you."

They were in the saddle the next morning at six A.M. moving north. Spur had picked out a pair of mounts the night before, got the rest of his supplies for a week's ride and packed the food and gear on his horse. He still wasn't sure that Robbie was going to be able to do the job.

By noon they had moved fifteen miles due north along the edge of the mountains in the near desert-like trail. They had passed Brigham City and continued north.

Once Spur thought someone was following them, but it turned out to be a lone rider who stopped at Brigham City.

A mile farther on, Robbie called another halt.

"Got to have something to drink," he said. "Not a drunk, but I just need a sip or two." He stepped down from his horse and slumped under a pine tree where they were cutting into the edge of the hills.

Spur swung down, tied the horses and got out a cold meal of cheese and biscuits and a can of sliced peaches. They had just finished eating when Spur heard hootbeats and looked up to see someone riding toward them. The closer the rider got, the more he wondered if it was the same one he had seen earlier.

When the horse came up he saw that it was ridden by a girl. She was astride and wore jeans and a man's shirt and wide-brimmed hat. On her hip was a six-gun.

She stared down at the pair from a dark frowning face. Spur realized she was a half-breed, pretty in a dark way. The blue eyes gave her away.

"Hi, Robbie, heard you got lucky."

"Go away, Breed. We're going just fine."

"How long you think you can last, Robbie? You've been weaving in the saddle the last three miles."

"Lie! I'll make it."

"You have a bottle with you?"

Robbie looked away. "Course not, damn Breed. Get outa here!"

"Robbie, I know you. Bet my horse against yours you got a pint in each of them baggy pants legs."

"No!"

"Miss?" Spur said, walking toward her horse.

"Mr. Spur McCoy. It's nice to meet you. You're a United States Secret Service Agent here to rescue the four white girls from Spotted Tail up in Ute country."

Spur grinned. "So much for secrets. I didn't hear your name."

"Right." She jumped off the horse, darted toward the man on the ground and pulled a pint of whiskey from where his pant leg had been tied at his ankle. She threw it on a rock, shattering the bottle.

"Goddamnit nooooooooo!" Robbie wailed.

"Robbie, a person has to know who and what he is. You're not a guide. Get on your horse and turn it in at the stable. You'll probably get paid enough to go on another two week drunk."

Robbie looked up, still crying because of the lost pint. "You think Mr. McCoy might pay me a little?"

"He's a fair man, Robbie." She turned to Spur. "Mr. McCoy, my name is Istas, I am half Ute. I lived with the Utes when I was very young, and then again when I was twelve. They abandoned me the first time, I came back to Ogden when I was thirteen. I am not really wanted in either camp. But I know the hills. I can guide you to wherever Spotted Tail is making his winter camp."

"You still look thirteen. How old are you?"

"I have twenty-two summers."

"And you know the country, the language?"

"Yes."

Spur went back to his pack, sliced cheese and put it between halves of a roll and handed it to her. She inspected it, then ate with an undeniable hunger.

"Where would you go next, if you were my guide?"

"To Logan, another twenty miles into the mountains on the Logan river. There I will talk to any Indians or breeds I can find and see if they know which winter camp Spotted Tail is using."

Spur knelt down by Robbie. "Istas is right, Robbie. You never would have made it. Might have got us both killed out there. I'll pay you ten dollars for your time, agreed?"

Robbie nodded eagerly trying to figure out how many bottles of wine he could buy for that much.

Istas scowled. "That much wine all at once could kill him."

Spur took out a ten dollar greenback and tore it in half. He gave one half of it to Robbie. Then he wrote a note and gave it to the drunk.

"Give the note and the half a bill to your favorite bartender. I'll bring in the other half when I get back. I told the barkeep not to let you draw more than a pint every two days. That should keep you moving."

"But . . . but I need more . . ." He gave up, stood, and they helped him back into his saddle. Then Spur took the second pint from his other pants leg, and poured half of it into the dirt. He capped it and gave it to Robbie.

"Half a pint will get you back to Ogden." He looked at Istas. "If we have twenty miles to do yet today, we better hit the saddle."

She told him the story of her early life as they rode. They were more into the hills now and it was a little cooler.

"A white trapper operating in the hills near the camp raped my mother when she hunted for roots. I was the result. When it was certain that my eyes were blue and my skin so light, and my nose so much non-Ute, I was placed on a snowbank and left there to die. I was two years old at the time, but they bound my hands and feet. If it an old Indian custom in our tribe, used mostly for deformed babies."

"Somehow you got away," Spur said.

"No, I was rescued by another trapper, a man I grew to love as my own father. He may have been, I'll never know for sure."

"Ezekiel Smith," Spur said.

"Yes. How did you know?"

"A guess."

"He raised me until I was twelve. Then I told him I wanted to go back and live with my other people for a while. He said I would not like it there, the Utes were savages. He told me if I went I could never be his daughter again."

"Smith is a tough hombre."

"Now I know that. When I was twelve I didn't. So I lived with the Utes for a year. They tolerated me, but I was not accepted into the tribe as a full member. After a year I came back to Ezekiel Smith's house and he said he didn't know me, that I certainly was no daughter of his."

"But you must have been there last night when I talked to Mr. Smith."

"I was in the stable behind his house. Ruth was giving me supper. She sends word about once a week for me to come. Ezekiel would be furious if he knew. She is a kind person."

"She certainly is. A question. If you were with the Utes only for a year, how could you learn the area so well?"

"I was there the year of the long drought. We had to keep moving from one spring and water hole to the next, and from one small stream after the other. Everything but the Logan river went dry that year."

They worked deeper into the mountains and it soon became obvious that they would not get to Logan before dark.

"We will camp. I can get fresh meat for supper if you wish." She watched him closely for his reaction.

"Camp yes. Fresh game, no. We can eat what we brought, and restock when we're in Logan."

Spur sat and watched as she made camp. She cleared a small area under three big pines, then scraped through the needles to bare earth and quickly built a small cooking fire. She heated beans in the cans, and toasted the biscuits and made coffee. It was all ready sooner than he thought possible. They ate as the darkness came. She cleaned up the meal, dug a small hole for the trash and buried it, then built up the fire a little and pulled her blankets off her horse.

McCoy had already spread out his blankets. She put hers right beside his, then vanished into the brush for a moment. When she came back she lay down on her blankets and stared at the fire.

"Mr. McCoy, do you know how I live? I clean out the stables, and the owner gives me a place to sleep. He does not pay me. Sometimes customers will give me a dime or a nickel. If they don't I have to steal to eat. Do you think it's wicked to steal in order not to starve?"

"No, Istas. I think it is wicked to put a thirteen year old girl out into the street. I think it is wicked to let you clean out the stable and not pay you. It is wicked that a closed society like the Mormons would permit a person to be treated this way."

"You are very kind, too, like Ruth. But to the Mormons I am not a person. Not even my soul can be saved. I am not a person, I am a half-breed."

Spur touched her shoulder. "Istas, you are a person. You are worth a lot. You have dignity and purpose. Remember that." He took his hand back. "Now I think it's time we get some sleep. We have a long day tomorrow."

Istas sat looking at the tall man who had befriended her, and touched her, and said wonderful things about her. Now he lay down and turned his back. He must think she was a person, but an ugly person. She had fully expected that he would want to take her clothes off and use her body. For just a moment a soft smile slid over her face. Then she sighed. There would be many more nights on the trip. She would wait and see.

When morning came, Spur sat up and looked around. The girl was not beside him. Her blankets were rolled and tied to her saddle. He smelled coffee and frying bacon. He had forgotten the slab of bacon that would spoil today if they didn't use it. She had fried the bacon in a small tin skillet from his pack.

"Bacon, bread and cheese," she said, setting a tin plate beside him. "There is a can of pears. Do you want them now?"

He didn't realize he was so hungry. He nodded. She brought the can and opened it with her own knife, then sat down on the grass and ate and drank the coffee she had brewed.

"We're about three miles from Logan," Istas said. "I should ride in behind you, so no one will know we're together. It will be easier for you."

They made arrangements to meet on the far side of the bridge over the Logan on the trail north, then he set out for Logan. It was smaller than he had thought, and the sign said the elevation was a little over 4,500 feet. The air was crisp for September. He found a mercantile and bought a small sack of staples, but said little, and realized the store owner asked few questions. This was not a wildly talking town.

When he came outside Spur heard a gunshot. He saw people running on the street toward the sound.

He ran too. When he was halfway there he heard one man shout to another that somebody had shot down a halfbreed.

CHAPTER SEVEN

ORDERS FROM COMPANY F of the Fifth Cavalry under the command of Capt. Harley Landower were changed again. They had been working their way toward Ogden, but now shifted their route and settled down in a temporary bivouac on the west side of Bear Lake. They were in the edge of the hills they swept down to the impressive lake, under the fringes of pines and small hardwood trees.

Lt. Joseph Windsong was just as happy about the change. He was trail weary, as garrison greenhorns usually are. And the stop would give him a chance to work on his plan for revenge and to regain his good name.

The last two days he had performed with spit and polish and authority on the march and in camp. Captain Landower had not spoken to him except on official business—but there had been no more ass chewings. He was gaining a little more respect with the troopers.

The strict separation in social status of enlisted versus officer was a tradition of long standing. Almost all enlisted men disliked or hated their officers—simply because they were officers. It was to be expected. To reach an understanding with an enlisted man was doubly hard, except through the cauldron of a tough battle.

Lt. Windsong expected one soon. Just as soon as he could find out enough about where the Indians were camped. He was working on it. Last night just after dark when the camp had been set up, he sent a scout of his own out looking for Ute signs. It was a secret mission that he paid the trooper five dollars for. That was nearly half a month's pay.

Now, Lt. Windsong settled down in his tent with the company scout, Lawson Kirk. The man was close mouthed and intensely concerned about finding the Utes and his daughter.

"Then you understand my position, Mr. Kirk?"

"Yep. I been around the army long enough to know how it is. If you don't do something spectacular soon, your ass is gonna be kicked out of the service."

"I would resign, sir!"

Kirk stood an inch from the officer, his chin jutted out and fire flittered dangerously in his eyes.

"Look, you slimy coward! Don't ever talk to me with that tone of voice again, or I'll slit your throat! You understand me?"

Windsong took a step backward, his own eyes wide with surprise and sudden fear.

"Yes, sir. Of course. I've been under a lot of pressure lately . . ."

Kirk stepped back, too. "Yeah, okay. Guess I

shouldn't have popped off that way. Just don't pull that phony officer superiority shit on me. I know better."

"Mr. Kirk. I see it this way. You and I have to find the Utes before Captain Landower does, or before he knows we have. Then we move in with half the company on a *patrol* and wipe out the savages, retake the hostages and get back to the railroad."

"I know what you want to do, save your ass. I know what I want to do. What I'm not sure is what Capt. Landower will do. If he won't attack, and it looks possible, I'll work with you. I can't promise a thing. But I'll keep my eyes and ears open."

"I could make it worth your while, Mr. Kirk."

The scout came to his full height and stared at the officer. "You say that once more and I'll jam it right down your young, pampered, sissy throat! Don't push your luck." He turned and marched out the tent flap.

Lt. Windsong relaxed in his folding chair and smiled. He had made a good ally, who would help him, he was sure. Touchy, but a man who knew what he was doing. When the raid came, Mr. Kirk would want to lead it, Lt. Windsong was sure. He smiled. The man leading a raid often was one of the first killed.

A half hour later, Captain Lawson called a meeting of his top noncoms and his officer. They looked at a map. Two areas had been circled, one near Ogden in the mountains, another ten or twelve miles from the southern end of Bear Lake.

"We think the hostiles are in this area," Captain Lawson said, pointing at the Bear Lake area. "In the next two or three days we will send out patrols to probe gently watching for signs. I'll lead the first patrol, and Mr. Kirk will advise. If we need a second patrol, Lt. Windsong will lead it. We will go in more force, twenty-man units. It will be harder to move undetected, but such a force will mean that a small band of hunters or some roving braves will be less likely to attack us. Are there any questions?"

Sgt. Bennedict spoke first. "Will we engage, or simply try to find where this winter camp is located?"

"We will not engage the enemy unless we are attacked with no option for a quick withdrawal. We are not here on an extermination mission. We are looking for the four white girls. Some tribes kill all hostages the first few seconds after they are attacked by the army. It serves a double purpose for the hostiles.

"It discourages the army attacking tribes with hostages, and by killing the hostages it relieves the Indians of having to guard them during an attack or withdrawl."

Lt. Windsong spoke up. "So we reconnoiter, map our position, our trails in and out, and record the location of any savages seen."

They went on talking for twenty minutes, the enlisted men concerned with length of the patrols, whether they should take food and supplies for one, two or three days, and how any shortage of supplies or ammunition should be handled.

They were told to use the supply wagon to bring every man up to regulations on equipment, and to charge any not in a fire fight for lost equipment or expended rounds.

"Are there any further questions?" Captain Landower asked. There were some minor ones and the group was dismissed.

"Mr. Kirk, I would like a word with you," Captain Landower said.

A few minutes later in the captain's tent, the commander poured a shot of whiskey in a tin cup for the sutler and scout.

"Can you tell me what's going on in my camp?" Landower asked.

"Sir?"

"Last night, Lt. Windsong sent out a trooper to scout around the area. Do you know why?"

"He hasn't told me why he did that," Kirk said, starting to feel like he was caught in the middle.

"Any ideas?"

"Only idea I'd have you already thought of, Captain. He's got his tail burned, his career is probably in trouble, and he might be looking for some way to do something to save his ass."

"That's what I figured." Landower rubbed his face with a big hand and slashed it back through his red hair. "Well, he won't have a chance to do much on his own. I'll lead every patrol we need until we find the Utes and set up some kind of a parley. This isn't a prelude to another Indian massacre."

"When's the first patrol?"

"Tomorrow, Mr. Kirk. We'll leave at dawn.

I'll pass the word about noon so the men can have plenty of time to get ready."

"Could I make a suggestion, Captain?"

Lawson nodded.

"Take forty men, not twenty. That will leave sixty troopers in camp, and give us a workable force that would put a caution into a dozen Ute warriors on the prowl. They don't like to fight when the odds aren't even or in their favor."

"Done. That's what the army pays you for, Mr. Kirk. Thanks. Well, I have a report I need to write so it will be ready if we touch the railroad again."

Kirk got up, waved and left the tent. He walked to his bedroll, got a towel and went down to the lake where he stripped and dove in. He had brought soap and enjoyed a bath before his swim. The water was colder than he expected, must still have had some snow-melt runoff into it.

Kirk splashed for half an hour, then lay on his towel in the sun to dry and got back to camp in time for the noon meal. They had fresh cooked navy beans and the last of the beef. After today it would be back to beans and hardtack, maybe coarse bread once a week.

Just before the announcement was made to the troops about the patrol the next morning, Lt. Windsong was told. He knew it was an intended slight. He should have been told as soon as the captain decided. He ignored it, and planned with his commander what precautions should be taken in the captain's absence. It would be a two day patrol of forty men, not twenty. Sgt. Bennedict would remain as Lt. Windsong's top enlisted man.

In the afternoon the troops were given permission to swim in the lake in two shifts, as long as guards were posted. Lt. Windsong swam as well, naked like the rest, diving in and swimming out a hundred yards with a steady crawl, then turned and came back with a leisurely side stroke.

He felt refreshed and ready when he dressed. Two days. His mind was whirling. He would find the areas that the captain's group would search, and he would lead a small *security* patrol of his own in another direction. They would be gone only during the day, but cover a lot of territory.

Lt. Windsong smiled. Yes, things were shaping up. He would have surprises for both Captain Landower and Sgt. Bennedict. He saw the sergeant's face and heard his taunts about being in the army for twenty years. He snorted. The sergeant would never make twenty-one years.

Spur McCoy heard the talk that someone had shot a halfbreed and ran faster. He had stopped in Logan for supplies with Istas, the half-Ute girl. Now he feared for her life.

He ran ahead of the others, came around a building and saw several people staring down at a small form lying in the dust of the street. Spur drew his .45 and blasted a shot into the air.

The gawkers around the body pulled back. One man stood holding a six-gun pointed at the ground. Spur could tell that the man was drunk.

A moment later Spur saw that the form was indeed Istas, and charged the drunk, slamming two roundhouse blows into the man's jaw, jolting him to the ground. Spur kicked away his old Colt and turned to the girl.

She sat up, her face showing pain, blood splotching her right sleeve. Spur pulled back the shirt from her lower arm and saw where the bullet had grazed her.

"Just one shot?" Spur asked.

She looked up, smiled at him and nodded. "Just one."

Some of the people were surprised when she spoke English. Spur turned to the gunman and was ready to kick him down the block when a small man with a badge pushed through the crowd. He took in the situation at a glance and looked up at Spur.

"You know this Injun?"

"The lady is Istas and she's my guide. I want you to throw that man in jail and charge him with attempted murder."

The sheriff went over to the man in the dirt, picked up his gun and helped the man stand. He brushed him off, gave him back his gun and talked to him quietly for a minute.

"You're not going to arrest him?" Spur asked.

"Didn't break any law. An Injun isn't a person in Logan. The Utes hit some cabins few miles out of town last week, killed two women, raped three more and got away clean. One of the women killed was Ted Nance's wife. He ain't over it yet." He paused and looked at Spur again. "Don't I know you?"

"Probably not, Sheriff. I never been to Logan before. And if this is the reception you give strangers, I'll probably never come here again."

"That suits Logan just fine. Now get your baggage out of town. You just got time to get your horses, otherwise I'm charging you both with disturbing the peace."

Spur stared at him for a moment concealing his anger. A typical small town sheriff, even if he was a Mormon. "Thanks for your help, Sheriff. I never forget a kindness. Which means I don't have much to remember from my visit to Logan." A woman gasped at his remarks. Istas had stood up and walked with Spur down the street to her horse.

The sheriff walked behind them. Istas swung up on her mount, and a few minutes later Spur mounted his own horse which he had left by the emporium. They rode north out of town and across the bridge over the Logan river.

"Friendly little place," Spur said.

"It's always this way right after an Indian raid. When will my people learn that they can't fight the white man?"

"That will take a long time, Istas. It was your land first. We're the invaders. If England or France or Spain tried to put settlers on California or in Oregon, we certainly would fight."

They rode in silence for a while. "It's the same, Mr. McCoy, but it is also different. The

Utes are nomads, hunters and fighters. They will never understand what it means to *own* a piece of ground a hundred feet square."

A mile up the trail north they stopped and he washed out the wound with whiskey. As the alcohol touched the raw flesh she winced but didn't cry out.

Spur grinned. "I've seen two hundred pound men faint when they get a wound splashed with alcohol that way."

"I cried inside," she said.

He bound up the groove in her arm, tearing down the end of the makeshift bandage and tying the ends together to secure it.

She told him what she found out in town before the drunk had shot her.

"The Ute raiding party was a few renegades who Spotted Tail had put out of his tribe. I heard in town that Spotted Tail has moved to his new winter camp which is farther from any road or settlement. He hopes it will be safer there. It's about ten or twelve miles from Bear Lake."

"How far is that from here?"

"Cross country, Bear Lake is about twenty-five miles. There is a horse trail that leads north more and then east, but it is ten miles longer and comes out at the middle of the lake where there is a settlement."

"What's your suggestion?"

"We follow the trail for about ten miles, then go due east cross country toward the lake. My guess is Spotted Tail's winter camp is back up one of the streams that feeds the lakes from the mountains. The rougher the hills and mountains, the closer we should be to Spotted Tail."

"Let's do it." He looked over at her. She held the reins with her left hand.

"Is that arm all right? Is it hurting?"

She looked up at him and her face broke into a glorious smile.

"Yes, it hurts, but I keep that inside." She looked away and tears touched her eyes. "Thank you, Mr. McCoy. You were concerned about me. Nobody but Ruth has ever been worried about how I am."

"High time somebody was," Spur said.

They rode a little faster, and within two hours she pointed to the east. They left the scratch trail and moved into the timbered and wooded slopes. The growth was not thick, but there was a certain amount of trail and direction selection. Spur held back and let her lead the way. She flashed him a bright smile, happy to take the responsibility.

After another hour Spur called a halt. They had been working up the side of a serious slope, and stopped where a bright chattering stream worked its way down a narrow valley.

"Dinner time," Spur said. The sun was high overhead and they found some aspens and pines to sit under near the brook.

"Fire?" she asked. "It is safe here, plenty far from the Ute camp yet."

Spur nodded. He used the small cooking fire she built so he could cook the two steaks he had brought.

"Spoil in another day," he said. "Just had a hankering for a good steak."

She found potatoes he had brought and caked them with mud, then pushed them into the coals to bake.

In twenty minutes they had their meal. She boiled coffee and they sat watching the fire and eating the steak and chewing on biscuits spread with marmelade he had picked up in the store.

"I am eating too much," she said. "I will grow big and fat."

He looked at her slender body with its more than adequate curves and laughed.

"I couldn't imagine you getting fat."

She moved closer to him. "You are so kind to me. I want to thank you. You make me feel like a person again, the way I did when I lived as daughter of Father Smith."

The food was gone, the tin plates set to one side. For just a moment she leaned in and her shoulder touched his.

"You are an important person, Istas. No matter what some say, you are of great value and worth. You are a human being, exactly like the rest of us."

She leaned against him now and tears flooded her eyes. He put his arm around her and let her cry. She was through in a minute and she looked up, smiling through the tears that were still there.

"Mr. McCoy . . ."

He held up his hand. "Istas, please call me Spur."

She nodded. "Spur, you have been so kind to

me. Made me feel so good. If there is . . . could I do anything . . ." She at last shrugged and unbuttoned the fasteners on the man's shirt she was wearing. It was much too large for her and in a moment she had it open and pushed off her shoulders revealing her torso and her handful sized soft brownish breasts.

"Spur, I would be so happy if you would love me."

He watched her, saw the intense honesty in her eyes, the wanting deep in her serious expression.

"You don't have to, Istas. I promise that I won't touch you on this whole trip. So don't think that you need to do this."

"For you I don't need to. But for me, I have a strong need, Spur. Never has a man really made love to me. Many have taken me roughly, hating me as they use me, but never in respect and joy and friendship . . . or love."

She reached for his leather vest and unbuttoned it, then opened his shirt and helped him take it off. She smiled and leaned in and put her cheek against the black hair on his chest.

"You have a marvelous body, Spur McCoy!"

She unbuttoned the fly of the men's jeans she wore and pulled them off, then took down her soft white cotton drawers, and sat there in the grass, dappled by sunlight through the tree branches. She was beautiful, calm, composed, serene and inevitably giving him the sexiest feeling.

Spur pulled off his pants and short underwear and sat beside her.

Then she gave a small cry of need and moved on top of him, pushing him flat on his back.

"Spur McCoy, I have no right, but I love you!" Then she kissed him and Spur responded as he felt her hands at his crotch grasping his already stiffening phallus.

The kiss was short, then she kissed his whole face, his eyes, nose, cheeks and neck. She lifted higher so her breasts hung down and he moved her so he could kiss her orbs.

"Yes, I like that!" she said with a small squeal. He kissed them both again, sucked and chewed them until her hips began to grind and pound against him. She wailed and cried out in surprised joy and then shivered and vibrated as spasm after spasm of delight tore through her soft, small brown body.

She sighed and lifted up and looked at him.

"I'm sorry, I've never done that before, been first."

"I'm delighted that I could excite you that much. Don't be sorry, tell me you're glad, and happy, and that you are important in this world."

She smiled shyly, then moved up so her breasts teased his mouth again.

"I am glad you excited me, and I am happy and I am important in this world and I want to make things better between the Indians and the whites."

Spur pulled her down and kissed her mouth, pushing his tongue inside and then slowly turning her over, careful not to let all of his weight bear down on her. She sighed and when the kiss ended she had spread her legs and her hands had grasped him and was urging him into her wet and warm slot.

"Yes, Spur, please now. I can't stand it another minute without you coming inside me!"

Spur moved then, and adjusted the thrust forward. She cried out in surprise and joy as he probed and stroked and then at last sank deeply into her to his own roots.

"Oh . . . oh . . . oh . . . so delightful! So marvelous!"

Then to Spur's surprise her intense emotion had surged his own and almost at once he pounded his hips at her furiously. In ten strokes he had drained his load deep inside her, and his breath came like a tornado as he tried to recapture some of his lost strength.

When his windstorm breathing returned to normal, she reached up and kissed his nose.

"Love me again, Spur McCoy," she said. "Make love to me again."

Three more times they lay in the grass on the soft forest floor and loved. Then they both splashed each other with the cold water from the little stream and dried in the sun.

"Let's just stay here tonight," Spur said. "This little glen has beautiful memories for me." They didn't bother to dress. She fixed up the little camp, moving round like a naked nymph. He sat and watched her. Then she came and sat beside him, pushing her feet and legs into the cold water.

"My life has changed here," she said. "I'll have to leave Ogden, but I will go where I can help the Indian people. Somehow I can show them that I am a *Squaw In Two Camps*. That will be my Indian name, and I will be able to help both my people to live in peace."

They talked about what she might be able to do, and Spur said he would try to get her a job in the government, something to do with the Indian agency. It was worth a try. Who would know more about Indian/white problems than Istas? He warned her that he could promise nothing, but he hoped he could find some place where she could fit into the government.

They had a leisurely dinner, told each other about their early lives, and then slowly, deliciously, they made love once more, this time under the stars. Then they went to sleep.

CHAPTER EIGHT

THE SECOND DAY Istas and Spur rode steadily
until midday. By then they had climbed the long
slope to a pass in the mountains, and turned
north again taking the downslope easily. Three
times they stopped and Istas either sat on her
horse or climbed a tree and studied the sur-
rounding territory.

Once she came back reporting that she had
seen two Ute hunters running through the trees,
moving after a small herd of deer. The Utes
could not be more than three days walk from
their camp if they had no horses.

Late that afternoon they came upon an abandoned camp. Istas studied it carefully, found
some arrowheads and broken pottery. She said
the Utes had been gone for nearly two months.
This had been a summer berry and fish camp.
They probably had left for their winter lodges
higher in the hills.

They ate a cold supper. Istas had found some
late blooming berries, and a root she dug that
tasted like wild onions. With the rest of the
bread and the last tin of applesauce it completed
their meal.

Later they arranged camp and put down their sleeping blankets. Istas took off her shirt and washed it in the small stream, hung it on some bushes to dry and walked back to Spur bare but totally at ease. She sat beside him and waited until he looked at her. Only then did she speak.

"Spur, for as long as you want me or need me, I will be your woman. I am love-bound to protect you since we both made love willingly. Now you can trust me with your life in this Indian land. A time may come when we are too close to Spotted Tail's camp to make love freely." She opened his fly and carefully worked out his erection.

Gently she smiled, and kissed his lips, then bent and took him in her mouth easily and with tenderness. Spur had never been partial to oral lovemaking, but now he reviewed his stand. After a few moments she had him on his hands and knees over her as she took his whole sturdy length into her mouth and throat and built his anticipation so high that he was afraid he would hurt her as his fires built higher and higher.

Her hands found his scrotum and her fingers danced around his testicles like lightning strokes.

Spur was panting now as she worked his pitch higher yet and he screamed when he climaxed, a long primal roar, echoing through the trees, as if a warning to all other males to stay their distance while he was in heat.

He collapsed to one side and his *mini death* lasted longer than usual. She was beside him when at last he had quieted his gasping for breath and his racing heartbeat.

"Who taught you to do that so well?" he asked.

She laughed quietly and snuggled against him. "No one taught me. I am a woman, I know."

"The same way you know where to find berries so late in the season, the way you know where the edible bulbs and roots grow, the way you know how long a tribe has been gone from a camp, the way you always find a small stream for our night camp?"

"I am half Indian woman, so I know."

He reached over and kissed her lips. She made a small sound and kissed him back three times, quick little love kisses. Her hand came up and stroked his cheek.

There were tears in her eyes again.

"Spur, you are the glorious lover I never had, you are the marvelous, tender husband I never will have. You are my love-life pushed and jostled and crammed into a few short days. So I must take advantage of it as much as possible. Somehow I don't expect a long life. I never have. First, I should have died in that snowbank.

"That was why the Indians named me Istas, which means *snow*. Then I should have died when I came back from the tribe, and Father Smith turned me into the streets. I almost did die, but I held on. Now I know why!" She reached up and kissed him again, then pulled one of his hands to her breasts. "Darling Spur!

Please love me right now before I burst with happiness!" She saw the look in his eye.

She caught his other hand and brought it to her crotch. "Use three fingers, but push them into me now!"

They slept little that night. Every two hours she roused him and they made love again. Spur was amazed at how she could time it so well, how she could know that he would be ready again. When the sun came up she jumped off the blankets and began making breakfast.

She made coffee on a tiny smokeless fire that could not be detected more than twenty feet away. He knew the principle, use dry wood that doesn't smoke at all, but he had never seen it done so well. They chewed on dried beef and two rolls Istas found in the food sack.

Soon they were in the saddle, moving north. By ten that morning Istas held up her hand for him to stop, a finger over her lips. They sat totally still as a lone Ute brave ran toward them, then slanted slightly downhill, his eyes on the tracks in the soft carpet of leaves and needles under the tall pine trees.

If the Indian had glanced uphill he would have seen them. Spur eased the hammer down on his .45 as the brave jogged past. He was moving at a pace that would eat up six miles an hour. Like most Indian braves he probably could keep going that way for ten hours without stopping.

She watched Spur, but still held up her hand. They sat for another five minutes before she motioned him up beside her. They had reached the slope of a small valley that opened into a larger one. Just at the horizon they could see a shimmer of blue.

"Bear Lake," she said pointing. "I don't think Spotted Tail would have his main winter camp on a valley this small. The hunger is ranging out, checking on game as well as killing it. I'd guess two or three ridges north."

"Should we set up a base camp and hide the horses and move on foot?"

She smiled. "You have stalked Indians before, Spur McCoy. But this is Indian work. We find a safe camp in some thick brushy area, and then I will make the scouting trips and see what I can find."

"I am going with you."

"No. I am only half Indian, so it will be twice as hard for me to get close enough to be sure where the camp is. With both of us it would be impossible." She smiled. "That would be one and a half whites."

"Let's find a camp, then we'll fight about it."

Two hours later they found a good place to hide their horses and their camp. It was near a small stream, and clogged with brush and tall grass and a heavy stand of young pine trees. A Ute would have to stumble over their horses to see them. A thin, no smoke fire would dissipate in the branches of the small pines, if it were built correctly.

He had shown her how to tie the tails of the shirt so it would not snag on the brush. They both drank from the stream and looked at each other.

"This is my job and I'm going with you to scout out the Ute main camp. That discussion is ended."

"There are three hours of daylight left. We both can go looking for the Utes. I think we're still too far away, so there should be little danger, at least for now."

"Shall I take the rifle?"

She shook her head. "No. One rifle shot sound will travel for ten miles in these hills. It would bring Ute warriors from all over. In a situation like this, we Ute Indians use the old ways, bow and arrow and snare. Our rifles are for war, not for hunting." She frowned then lifted her brows. "I wish I could talk you into leaving your six-gun here as well, but then you don't have a bow and arrow to defend yourself with."

"We'll compromise. I'll take my Colt forty-five."

From somewhere in her saddlebags, Istas brought out a pair of well worn Indian moccasins. She took off the men's boots she had been wearing that were too large for her. She smiled as she slipped into the Indian footwear. She reached in the bag again and brought out a simple brown buckskin robe. She shucked out of her shirt and pants, but left on her cotton drawers. She pulled on the buckskin robe and tied it close around her neck.

"If they spot us I could pass as one of them from a distance," she said.

An hour later they had moved quickly across two ridges on the side of the mountain, but still they could see no sign of the Indian winter camp. They paused below a thick stand of pine and brush and looked down in a third valley. It was twice as wide as the others they had seen, with a river twenty feet wide and brim full of snow melt even this late in the year.

He felt her tense where they touched lying on the soft forest mulch. Her hand came out and pointed. Below, a hundred yards from them, two Ute braves crouched. They stared away from the pair above, watching three deer feeding near a small stream. Both Indians lifted their bows and as if on signal, each loosed arrows at the same deer, a six point buck which had just lifted his head to turn in their direction.

The hunters were thirty yards from their target, but both arrows penetrated the torso, just in back of the front legs, aiming for the heart. The big buck tried to rear up. He kept watching the spot where he thought he had seen danger. But it was too late. A second pair of arrows darted through the air and hit the buck. He pawed the ground and went down, the two does with him scattered in opposite directions in fright.

"How much will that buck weigh, dressed out?" Istas asked in a whisper.

Spur whispered back. "About a hundred and forty pounds."

"So all we have to do now is follow them back to their camp. Would you wander around lugging seventy pounds of venison on your back?"

Quickly the Indians below draped the buck

deer over a sturdy bush and butchered it, cut it in half and each brave shouldered half of the carcass and began moving north, away from the watchers.

They followed as closely as they could safely, but dusk closed in before the hunters made it back to their camp. They had gone over another finger ridge and kept moving north.

Spur and Istas sat in the darkness and decided they would stay there overnight and continue in the morning. They had no blankets or food. Before darkness became total, Istas found two bushes of ripe berries and three edible roots. They both munched on the sparse food, went down a small draw to a brook and filled up on water, then searched for a thicket where they could sleep.

Istas borrowed Spur's hunting knife and quickly slashed down a mattress of pine boughs, then another dozen boughs which they pulled over them for a blanket. They cuddled together and before long both were sleeping.

Spur woke up several times, but quickly went back to sleep. In the morning he was rested and when the first light broke the darkness, they were up and moving north through the early dawn.

They moved cautiously, higher on the ridges than the hunters had been, hoping they would miss anyone coming out this new day for hunting. They saw no one for two hours, then they topped a ridge and looked over it.

Below, the valley was half a mile wide. To the east they could see the blue of Bear Lake. To the west were mists and a few clouds that had not yet burned off the top of the valley. Through the clouds Istas saw plumes of smoke rising straight up in the quiet, morning air.

"The winter camp," she said. "We've found it. What can we do now?"

"First we move as close to it as we can. Will they have lookouts all around the camp?"

"Not now. They don't expect trouble. They will have a few scouts watching long range areas, where the Pony Soldiers might come from."

"Good. Right now we're downstream. We need to come in from above the camp. They'll have the fewest guards and lookouts that direction."

"But first the horses."

"We go back and get them. How far is Spotted Tail's camp from here?"

"Five, six miles. The way we go it will be at least ten. If both of us go back we should be able to find where we left them."

Spur laughed. "I'm glad you're the Indian in this team."

The pool was dug and filled. Yates and Barlow stood looking at it. They were twenty yards upstream, so they could get a pool and still have enough fall to drain it. They had to build part of a wooden flume to get the water over a low place, and now they were ready.

Barlow had scooped another fifty shovels full of sand into the sluice, and he signaled and Yancy lifted the two foot wide gate that held back the water. It surged forward, a foot deep, racing down the twenty yards of flume and stream until it came to the next gate where it slanted into the sluiceway, and splashed against the new sand and gravel.

At first there was a little spillage, then the dam-like structure of the sand washed downstream and began hitting the baffles. Barlow prayed they did their work.

It took them nearly four hours of using the pool and filling it twice more and working the sand before Barlow was satisfied. They hadn't even looked at the baffles. Now they turned off the water and sat back as the last of the water drained down the sluice box and back into the creek.

"Should know soon," Barlow said sending a stream of brown juice into the water.

Yates looked up at the hillside above them. "Say we do hit some good color here, where'd it come from? Up there? Is there a solid wall of gold up there somewhere waiting for us to chip hundred dollar chunks off?"

"Now you're getting delirious, you old fart."

"Hell, just got to come from a damn mother lode somewhere."

"Yeah, and chances are just as good that it used to be there, and that was about a million years ago, and this dust is all that's left of the mother lode."

"Could be."

"Should we look at those baffles?" Barlow asked.

"Damn right!"

They scrambled to the first baffle on the sluice and looked in the riffle of water that remained behind the inch-high baffle.

"Look at that!" Barlow said, a catch in his voice.

There was dust there, wet, heavy gold dust plastered against the baffle, and falling down below it, forming a curving glitter of pure gold dust!

"Lordy! Must be more than an ounce right there in that one place!" Yancy shouted.

They moved down the sluice. Each of the baffles looked about the same, loaded with gold dust!

Yates sat down heavily on the stream bank. "Land 'O Goshen! Must be near an ounce of dust on each baffle! Twenty four of them critters, I nailed them in. That's . . . good Lord! That's more than a pound and a half of dust! What's dust worth?"

Barlow laughed. "You old coot! Gold is the same price it's been since 1837. It's twenty dollars and sixty-seven cents an ounce. That's a little over three hundred and thirty dollars a pound."

Yates shook his head. "Land 'O Goshen! I swear. I never seen anything like this." He caught his breath, reached down to steady himself when a blackness swept over him, then he shook his head and felt fine.

"Well, you old coot! You just gonna sit there, or do you want to help scrape out the gold dust and put it in that jar you've been saving?"

"I'll go up and get it," Yates said.

Barlow handed it to him. "Brought it down yesterday. Been sitting here waiting all day. Clean and dry. Go ahead. Hit that first baffle and clean it out. You still got that inch-wide putty knife?"

"Right here somewhere." He found it and went to the baffle and lifted the pure gold dust from its wet trap. As he finished the first one he stared at the gold in the jar.

"God in Heaven! I never really thought we'd find enough gold to keep us going even. Now we could earn our keep for the rest of our lives! Hell, we can go back up to Frisco and buy one of them little houses looking out over the bay."

He handed the jar and tool to Barlow, who cleaned out the next three baffles. Barlow watched Yates a minute, grinned and went on to clean the rest of the baffles. If the good sand and gravel held, they could have enough to live on in a week or so. *If* the gravel held.

He finished the cleaning. The quart fruit jar looked about half full. He might have to do a little sifting and sorting after it dried, but it looked ninety-nine percent pure gold dust. He put the lid on the jar and put it to the side in a hole he had dug with a board over it, then went back to the head of the sluice box and began shoveling more sand into the structure.

"Might check and see how the pond is filling up, Yates," Barlow called.

Yates sat where he had been. He didn't respond.

"Hey, you old coot! You getting hard of

hearing now, too? I said you can check on the pond."

Barlow frowned when he got no reply the second time. He put down the shovel and hurried down the twenty feet of creek to where Yates sat. He was bending forward as if examining something.

When Barlow touched Yates he fell sideways on the stream bank.

"My God, no!" Barlow shouted. He saw the staring eyes, the stilled body. He reached for the artery on the old neck, but could find no pulse.

Barlow sat down on the bank beside Yates and held his partner's head in his lap and cried.

When the tears stopped he looked at his long time friend.

"Yates, you old coot. Nobody ever had a better friend. Nobody ever had a better partner. I sure don't know what I'm going to do now."

He stared up at the sluice, the shovel, the water and the pond which he could see was full again.

"Hell, you'd want me to work it out. Somehow I just know that you'd want me to get all the dust out of here I can. Then I'll go back to Frisco and buy that little house and leave a rocking chair on the front porch for you to sit in. Sit in it just anytime you want to."

Barlow stood, looked at his friend for a minute. "I better get new sand in the sluice and turn on the water. Then I'll find a spot along here and fix you up a fine grave. Nothing fancy, but probably better than I figure I'll ever have. You just hold fast there, Yancy, and I'll be right back with you."

On the fringes of trees a hundred yards above the sluice, two Ute braves stood watching. They did not understand what had happened below, but they did know what the long wooden box and the shovels meant.

More men had come looking for the useless squaw clay. The shiny yellow metal that was good only for squaws to make trinkets from. Spotted Tail would want to know about this. He would want to know quickly.

One of the braves stayed to watch the small camp, while the other held his bow and three arrows in his right hand and began jogging back toward the winter camp. Spotted Tail would want to know about this as soon as possible since they were within two days walk of the winter camp.

CHAPTER NINE

SPUR MCCOY AND Istas walked the four miles back to their horses, broke their camp and rode north and west to get behind the Indian tepees. It was slow going for the horses, and late in the afternoon when they tied their mounts in heavy brush, and crawled up to a point where they could see the camp. Directly behind the tepees loomed a hundred foot sheer rock wall.

A thick stand a half grown pine trees crowded both sides of the river here. The watercourse was twenty feet wide, but appeared to be only knee deep where it gushed from the series of low falls just north of camp.

They had worked up to within a hundred yards of the backs of the closest tepees.

Istas lay in the grass watching the camp. "I see few braves. This is not normal. Most of the braves must be off on a hunt or on a raid."

"Maybe we could walk in and get the girls and leave, right now," Spur said.

"No. There are always a few braves left to guard the camp. Spotted Tail would never leave his women and children defenseless. The braves are there, we just can't see them."

"Maybe I can get one of the girls out."

"First we have to know where they are. When it gets dark I can move into the camp and listen for the girl and the gossip. If I'm lucky I can find out which braves own which girls and where they are. Then it will be easier."

"I don't like that plan."

"Why, because I'm taking the risk, and not you? Remember these are my people. I can pass in the dark. I don't want the army Blue Coats to come charging in and slaughter my whole tribe."

Spur sighed. "We'll wait. Maybe we can spot them in the daylight as well."

Normal activity around the camp had slowed, Istas said. One hunter came in with six big birds. Another came back with half a deer. He would return to get the rest of it before darkness.

A few squaws worked on clay pots, and then fired them in an open pit fire that looked white hot.

"There," Spur said suddenly, pointing. A white girl wearing no top came from a tepee, looked around and quickly ran into another one.

"Strange," Istas said.

Soon it was dusk, and Istas moved quietly toward the tepees. She had explained that if she were caught and they discovered who she was, she would simply say she had come back to see them again, to talk to her friends. But with the reduced activity, she didn't think that would happen.

100

Spur lay in the grass waiting. He had his .45 up and ready, but even six or eight braves against his six-gun would not be much of a battle for the Indians. He would not fire the weapon unless it was absolutely necessary.

McCoy guessed at the time. It was more than a half hour later when he thought he saw Istas move from one tepee to another. He waited another half hour and when he was becoming nervous about how long she had been gone, she touched his elbow. He jumped and she laughed softly.

"You didn't think I'd come back the same way I went in, did you?" she asked.

She waved him away and they began working back through the darkness of the woods toward their horses.

"All four girls are still there. The pretty blonde one is now the woman of Spotted Tail himself, and she is untouchable by the other braves. The young girl, who is either twelve or thirteen, I couldn't catch what the squaws were saying, is being treated more like a daughter than a slave. She is being saved for the brave who captured her.

"One of the Mormon girls is quiet and well behaved, but the second one is wild and rude and violates the tribal courtesy and even some of the taboos. If she keeps doing this, she could be in for some discipline by the squaws, beatings most likely with willow switches until her back is marked and bloody."

"So why are we leaving? Why not get the girls out now?"

"There are six braves there, and to get the girls we would have to fight the squaws. They would scream for the braves. We need some kind of support. An army would be great."

"Where did the braves all go?"

"Spotted Tail led thirty braves out this morning. His scouts report a column of Pony Soldiers with two wagons have camped near Bear Lake."

"Do they know how many troopers?"

She smiled in the darkness. "Indians are not very good with numbers. The brave who reported the army at first said a thousand. Then he said there were ten times his fingers. Which may be somewhere near right.

"A column of a hundred cavalry troopers. That might be what we need. It might be a good idea if we were to pay the army a surprise visit. The surprise is going to be on the major or the commanding captain when I take over his troops."

They found their horses and moved in a more direct route back to the ridgeline that formed the broad valley. They went around the Indians, then down to the open valley where they could ride with few dangers. Five miles down the valley they moved into some pines and camped for the night. Both were too tired to do more than spread their blankets and fall on them, their legs touching. Istas moved against Spur and went to sleep at once.

In the morning they rode early and found the army camp near the southern end of the big lake. They heard two rifle shots as they went past a lookout. They stopped for a moment and Istas put back on her white man clothes, and they rode on to greet an escort of three troopers sent to meet them.

A corporal saluted Spur, who returned the salute.

"Corporal Tennelle, Sir. Our commanding officer, Captain Landower, welcomes you to our camp. You and the lady are more than welcome to take breakfast with the captain."

"Thank you, Corporal. We would be delighted." He smiled and looked at Istas. "I hope army chow is better than it used to be."

Ten minutes later they rode into the military camp. It looked remarkably familiar to Spur who had served in the big war and had reached the rank of captain before he went back to Washington D.C. to work for the New York senator.

As soon as the two guests dismounted, a soldier took their horses and said they would be rubbed down and fed. They stood in front of an officer's tent, a wall affair about eight feet square. A medium sized man with flaming red hair and moustache stepped from the flap and smiled at them.

"Welcome to our camp. I'm Captain Landower, in command of this expedition. Won't you come in for some breakfast?"

Spur led the way as the captain stood to one side. Istas followed close behind him. Inside Spur turned to the officer.

"Captain, this is Istas, a friend of mine and my guide. She's from Ogden. I'm Colonel

McCoy, operating with special orders directly from the commander-in-chief."

Captain Landower looked up quickly. "Of course you have some documentation?"

Spur took out his wallet, pried apart two tinplate pictures and removed a folded sheet of paper which he gave the officer.

Landower read it, nodded and handed it back. "My unit is at your service, Colonel."

"Your orders were to appear to be showing the flag, but in reality you are to rescue the girls?"

"Right."

"What are your plans?"

"First we locate the hostiles' camp. Then we attempt to parley. The savages have attacked my men once. If they attack again we will fight. Our scouts are trying to locate their camp and their strength."

"Those who attacked your men were renegade Utes," Istas said. "They might have come from any of the small tribal units. Spotted Tail would not send his braves against you without cause."

"You have special knowledge of the Utes?" Landower asked.

"Yes, I am half Ute, I speak their language fluently."

"So you could parley with Spotted Tail?"

"Yes."

"Captain, you know where the Ute camp is, and know that he has not more than forty braves. There appears to be no gathering of war parties."

"Then let's ride up there and show our force and demand the girls back," Captain Landower said.

"It can't work quite that easy, Captain," Spur said.

"Why not? We can out gun him two to one."

"We're on his territory. We'd never get close to his camp. He would attack us with hit and run raids that would leave us bleeding and half our men down before we moved a mile. He knows we're here. He has war parties out watching every move we make."

"It would be best to go parley first," Istas said. "He knows me. I haven't seen him in several years, but he will remember me, and I speak the language. Talking is best right now. There is no reason anyone else needs to die."

"My job is to get the girls out of there, alive," Captain Landower said.

"You know what will happen if you attack the winter camp?" Istas said.

"I've heard they will kill all captives."

"They will," Spur said softly.

"Then it looks like we need to parley first."

A man came through the tent flap unannounced. He was Lt. Windsong, and he was drunk. He stared at Istas a moment, then tried to draw his Army Colt .45 which was not on his hip.

"Indians!" he screeched.

Two enlisted men burst through the door, grabbed the officer and dragged him out of the captain's tent.

"That's my cross for this mission, Colonel.

You have just seen that eminent family name Windsong in action. This is the general's idiot son, First Lieutenant Joseph Windsong. He's been confined to quarters. He drinks, and he's an outright coward. My problem. Where were we?"

"We make plans to parley, tomorrow or the next day, depending how soon we can make contact and arrange it."

"You have some ideas about how we can do that?" Captain Landower asked.

Spur McCoy looked around. "We can talk about that right after we have some breakfast. Is the mess still serving?"

Lt. Windsong found himself dumped inside his tent on the hard canvas floor. It served to sober him up a little. The captain had taken his entire supply of whiskey, but he had bribed one of the men to steal a bottle from the captain's hoard. Now even that route to a good drink was gone. He stared at the empty bottle.

Lt. Windsong took out a pad of paper and a pencil, sharpened it with his knife and began to write. Even in his sobering up state he was lucid and bright. He reminded himself he was not a stupid man. He was a Windsong!

He had to take a different tack to get what he wanted. What was that? He wrote down on the pad:

"Purpose: 1. To gain back his own honor and the respect of his men. 2. To perform in such a way that he could remain in the army, and be promoted one day to General!

"Problem: How did he attain these goals?

"1. By not drinking any more . . . Easy. He was out of whiskey.

"2. By operating strictly within the codes of conduct of an officer and a gentleman to get back in the good graces of his commanding officer.

"3. By performing some feat of daring and brilliance that would at once keep him in the army, perhaps even win him a commendation or a medal!

"4. How? Lead a detachment, defeat Spotted Tail in battle, and rescue the four captive white girls."

Lt. Windsong stared at the pad of paper for a long time. Then he sent word that he wanted Sergeant Bennedict brought to his quarters at once.

Back at the captain's tent, the three of them were eating a late breakfast of ground beef from a newly butchered steer, bread and large mugs of coffee. A knock sounded on the door. Captain Landower grunted and a sergeant came in and spoke softly to the officer. The captain nodded and the sergeant left. A moment later the flap lifted again and the scout came in.

Captain Landower made the introductions.

"Colonel McCoy, this is Scout Kirk. He knows these hills as good as most of the Utes. He also has a daughter captured by the Ute, which is mostly why he's along as scout. Mr. Kirk, this is Colonel McCoy and Istas."

Kirk waved at the colonel, said a few words in

the Ute tongue to Istas. She smiled, and replied briefly.

"The colonel will be with us for a while, Kirk. Actually he'll be commanding until we get the girls out. You'll take orders from him, or through me."

"Yep. I figured we was getting some high powered gent in. That damn senator knows how to twist tails in Washington, don't he?"

Spur grinned, poured the scout a steaming cup of boiled coffee and grinned.

"Indeed Senator Patterson is a highly influential man. I was in Washington for several years and had a nodding acquaintance with him. He's a good man to have as a friend."

"So when do we parley?" Kirk asked.

"Getting right to the point," Spur said. "Kirk, I think you and I are going to get along fine."

CHAPTER TEN

GERTRUDE SAT IN Running Deer's tepee in the Ute winter camp and sighed. She wished she had a kerosine lamp. These savages went to sleep when it got dark. Night was the best time.

She giggled. Running Deer lay sleeping, exhausted from his after supper sex bout with Gertrude. His two squaws snored on the far side of the tepee. She sat naked on the pallet, wishing the Indian brave had not gone to sleep so soon. She stood and wandered to the flap of the structure and looked out.

Two young braves, boys really about fifteen, headed into the brush to relieve themselves. She slipped out of the tepee and followed them. She stopped just inside the fringe of the brush and waited. They came back together, talking softly. When they saw her standing naked in the moonlight they were surprised, then curious.

She motioned to them to come forward. She had learned what aroused an Indian man. It wasn't a kiss, it was stroking the inside of his thigh. She reached down and rubbed the spot on both young braves and she saw them tense and stare at her big white breasts. Gently she took one boy's hand and put it on her breasts.

She pushed past his loin cloth and played with his genitals and he yelped in pleasure. She caught both boys hands and led them deeper into the woods. Then she lay down on a grassy spot and pulled them down with her.

Young Indian boys were not promiscuous. The average young brave never had sex before he captured a woman from another tribe or until he took a wife. Both lay beside her hardly moving. She pulled off their simple coverings and played with their stiff, throbbing rods.

"Yes, boys, that's right," she said softly to them. "It isn't hard, it's easy." She lay before them and let them examine her, touch her wherever they wanted to. Suddenly one boy caught his penis in his hand and began to pump it back and forth.

She laughed and shook her head and pulled him on top of her. Gently she showed him what to do and where to place the throbbing head and then, with a cry of surprise, he penetrated her. She moaned in delight. His very first time!

At once the young brave shouted and climaxed. He pulled out of her quickly and jumped around the small clearing in what looked to Gertrude like a war dance. The other boy moved over her and a moment later he had lanced inside her and was pumping hard with his slender hips. Then he erupted and came away and did the same crazy little dance before vanishing toward the camp. She went back, surprised at this reaction to their first sexual encounter.

Gertude wandered around the camp a minute, well aware that squaws were not supposed to be out at night without some purpose. She saw no one else.

At one of the tepees she noticed a fire glowing inside and went up to it and looked through a small opening of the flap. Inside she saw a naked brave about to mount one of his squaws. The squaw must have seen movement at the door, because she screeched and pointed.

The brave jumped to the flap, caught Gertrude's wrist and pulled her inside. He had been drinking. The whole structure smelled of whiskey, probably a bottle they had taken from the train raid.

The brave looked at her and smiled. His hands fondled her big white breasts and he laughed. He reached and sucked on them and made a motion as though he were holding a baby. He pulled her down on the pallet and made her lower her breasts into his mouth so he could chew on them. The brave laughed, and as he chewed on her he began to masturbate.

His two squaws sat by and laughed. They frowned when Gertrude began playing with his erect phallus, and then shrieked when she pulled him down on top of her. When he entered her she wailed as he pounded his loins at her. The squaws scratched Gertrude and clawed her with jagged nails. He pushed them away, then hit them to drive them back as he exploded. He pulled away from the white woman and pushed her roughly out the flap of the tepee.

She sat on the ground where she fell, rubbing her bruises and scratches.

Then Gertrude snorted. "I guess I showed those old squaws how to take care of a brave!" She stood up and began to roam the camp to see what else she could find happening.

There was nothing. The other tepees were silent and dark. She went back to Running Deer's quarters and built up the fire a little and sat watching it. Running Deer had no sons by his squaws, but he did have one daughter who was about fourteen.

Gertrude's eyes glinted in devilment and anticipation. Quietly she went to the far side of the tepee where the girl slept. She woke her silently and urged her to come to the other side of the fire. Gertrude and the girl got along well. The girl felt sorry for Gertrude she was sure. Now she took advantage of that emotion and drew her down by the fire. In the still warm weather most of the Indians slept naked. The girl who was called Honey Bee was in the buff. She was slender with small breasts and almost no hips yet and a flat face with a curious expression. Her long black hair trailed down her back.

First, Gertrude smiled a lot, then she took Honey Bee's hands and put them on her own big, white breasts. The girl pulled back, but Gertrude smiled and nodded. When the first strangeness passed, Honey Bee became interested. She stared at her breasts and examined them, curious about the hard, erect nipples.

Slowly Gertrude touched Honey Bee's breasts. At first she pulled back, then as Gertrude smiled and nodded she understood and let the older girl feel her. It took only a minute of petting to bring new life to the small nipples as they enlarged and hardened.

The Indian maiden was surprised, but not alarmed.

Gertrude slowly began to seduce her, moving her hands over the young Indian girl's body, then massaging the inner thighs. Again she put Honey Bee's hands on her white body, trailing them down to her crotch and her spread legs. The ploy worked and as Honey Bee felt and watched her, Gertrude did the same to the Indian girl. Her fingers found her crotch.

It only took her a short time to find the soft, moist nether lips. Gertrude stroked the swollen clit and in another minute, Honey Bee climaxed with a long low cry and a series of spasms that shook her. When she finished she hugged Gertrude, watching her closely, then moved her hand down to Gertrude's crotch and toyed with her, then found her clit and fingered it until Gertrude exploded with a long wail and a climax of her own.

Three times they took turns with each other, then Gertrude sensed someone behind her. She felt a blow on the side of her head and tumbled across Honey Bee near the fire. The roar from Running Deer woke half the camp. He screamed at Gertrude and beat her on the head and shoulders.

When his rage had spent itself, Running Deer tied Gertrude with stout rawhide strips around the ankles and wrists, then tied her feet to a side tepee pole. Running Deer mumbled to himself as he built up the fire and sat in front of it, shouting a word now and then, staring at her, and getting furious all over again.

When morning came, Running Deer still sat in the same position. Gertrude knew she was in deep trouble. She had played around with other braves, and Running Deer had only laughed. She had seduced one of the sub chiefs who came to eat with them, and Running Deer had been proud of the sexual prowess of his captive wife.

But not now. He still glared at her. There was no way she could ask him what the matter was. She knew about homosexuality. But she did not consider fingering another girl to be that.

Maybe the Indians did!

Maybe the Ute's had a strict taboo against that!

Gertrude shivered for the first time. Just as the sun rose, she drifted into a troubled sleep.

She awoke and then slept uneasily several times that morning. At noon someone untied her ankles and dragged her to her feet. Running Deer found she could not walk because of the tight thongs, so he dragged her to the council fire.

All the braves of the tribe were there, except the lookouts. The squaws sat to one side.

They put Gertrude on a flat rock near the fire

and made her sit down. Her hands were still tied. She had no idea what they were saying, but when she saw Running Deer stand and begin talking, she knew it was not good.

Running Deer spoke to the council quickly and with emotion.

"For three months I have cared for this white squaw. She has lived in my tepee, she has eaten my food. I have been good to her, beating her only when she deserved it.

"Now she has violated one of our strongest taboos. She has touched and fondled and excited my oldest daughter. She has done the man-thing and my daughter is marked for life! I demand that he council pass judgement on this white squaw, and that she be given the usual punishment for this outrage."

Running Deer sat down and others on the council spoke, saying that the white squaw was young, that she was good for a man to relieve himself in and that she had been loaned by Running Deer to any brave who asked for her.

Others spoke. One brave said he heard that the woman had been laying with the young boys, introducing them into the rituals of sex too early.

More comments were made. Every brave who wished to speak on the matter did, then they turned toward Spotted Tail. The chief remained seated as he spoke.

"The white captives are different from our squaws. They seem to demand more attention, wish to have sex more often, are softer and larger and less adapt at he usual skills of a squaw than our own women. They are in a strange place, trying to learn strange ways. Still they must know their place in our society and remain there. They must learn our laws and rules and obey them.''

He looked across the camp at his own tepee where Priscilla sat in the open flat of his abode watching the council.

"Running Deer has brought the gravest of charges. It is he who must decide what the verdict is to be. He knows best the circumstances, the situation. He knows the captive white woman best. If the honor of his name and his family has been blackened, then he will make one decision. If his anger has cooled, and he knows that there was no lasting damage done, no arm cut off, no eye plucked out, no sanity disturbed, then he will rule the other way. The council gives Running Deer the decision on his own charges.''

No one spoke around the council fire. Often such a serious decision would be made by the chief. Now and then there would be a show of opinions as the braves stood to be counted. But more often in Spotted Tail's small band, the ultimate decision was left to the family or the brave.

Everyone in the council turned to look at Running Deer. There was no custom or law obliging him to make a decision. He could simply walk away from the council and take no action on his own charges. He could ask the council for one or two days to confer with the great spirits. Or he could give an immediate decision.

Running Deer stood and walked around the center of the council fire itself, staring into the embers. Then he went back to his place and remained standing.

"We are harrassed by the Blue Coats. Our young men fly off into the mountains to establish small tribes of their own. It is time we held by the old ways, followed the old laws and rules. It is a time for firmness with our own people, as well as against the Pony Soldiers.

"I say that this wanton, this unnatural one must undergo the test of the boiling blood."

None of the braves was shocked or surprised. It was a usual punishment for such a crime. It was expected. Some even hoped for it. The ritual would take place at once, leaving the braves free to be ready for a Blue Coat attack, or for war.

Running Deer signaled and his two squaws ran to the edge of the council area. He lifted the girl from the rock and took her to the squaws. One of them spit in her face. The other slapped her twice and laughed at her. Then they walked her to the end of the council fire where three poles with the tops tied together, formed a tepee without a covering.

The braves sat still. A loud wailing call came from one of Running Deer's squaws. At once the tepee emptied of women and children who sat around the far end of the council area in assigned locations.

117

One of the squaws built a small fire under the three poles. A second took a strong braided rawhide rope and threw it over the tops of the poles. A young boy climbed the pole and placed the rawhide rope so it fell into a groove that had been greased with venison fat so the rope would slide back and forth across it easily.

Running Deer went to where Gertrude slumped in the dirt. He sat cross legged in front of her and told her in detail what she had done and what the punishment was. She understood none of it. Her usual self assured smirk had changed to one of wonder and worry. When Running Deer dragged her under the three poles, and tied her feet with the rawhide rope, she screamed.

"No! You can't do this. It's inhuman! Don't let them do this to me!"

Her screams continued and the three white girls who had been forced to come to watch the *punishment* covered their ears to avoid hearing her cries.

"No! You're savages! I want to go home! Don't let them do this to me. Priscilla, make them stop!"

Priscilla turned her head but could still hear her name being called. She was not yet sure what was going to happen, but the death fear in Gertrude's voice, made her own blood chill to freezing.

Slowly the slack was taken up in the rope sliding over the greased top of the poles until Gertrude hung upside down, her head three feet off the ground. Her hands were lashed to her sides with rawhide, her old doeskin robe tied to her legs below the knees.

Running Deer had returned to his place in the council.

The squaws became more serious. The rawhide rope was loosened from the sturdiest pole and Gertrude was raised until her head hung four feet off the ground. Another rawhide strip was used to tie her long blonde hair tightly to her neck to prevent it falling lower than her head.

Running Deer looked and gave a hand signal. The squaw who had built the small fire moved it directly under the upside down girl. It was little more than a few charred sticks at first, but wisps of smoke curled upward and Gertrude bellowed her fear and anger.

Slowly the squaw added small sticks to the fire until it began to burn with a low flame. Gertrude shook herself to swing away from the rising smoke and heat. But the second squaw stopped the swinging. Gertrude coughed.

"Get me down from here!" she screamed. "I'll leave your little boys alone. Why didn't you tell me they were so touchy about the kids!" She coughed again and screamed.

The squaw put slightly larger sticks on the fire now, letting the flames jump up a foot from the ground. The heat even at four feet over the fire was high. Tiny tendrils of smoke spurted from the top of her head where a single hair burst into flame.

Gertrude's screams were continual now. Her voice cracked but still she screamed.

The Indians watched with no emotion showing.

The three white girls turned their eyes aside, unable to watch the torture. One of them vomited.

The fire now was maintained at its foot high level. Two more single hairs burst into flame and died out. The older squaw went to the tied rope that held Gertrude and untied it, then lowered the body a foot toward the flames and heat.

Gertrude's screams came again, fainter now, her face a terrible mask of hatred and disbelief, of fury and desperation.

"The Blue Coats will come and kill you all!" Gertrude screamed.

She felt the intense heat of the fire below her. Then more of her low hanging hair sizzled into flames and poofed out. Again and again the single strands burned, then a lock of the hair near the side of her forehead burst into flames, and in twenty seconds all the hair on her head flashed into flames and was gone.

Gertrude did not faint. She held onto consciousness as a drowning man grasps a floating plank.

She screamed again, but her voice was now reduced to a whisper.

Slowly the top of her head turned a soft pink, then black from the soot in the flames.

The squaw went back to the rope and raised Gertrude six inches, then tied the rope off and settled down.

Spotted Tail watched the execution with calm

eyes. He had seen the ritual more than once, and knew it was one of the reasons the white men called them savages. But how was it that much more cruel than the white man's hanging, or an army firing squad? The final result was the same.

The girl should have been spared. She had a delightful body that had given pleasure to half the braves in camp. But he could not interfere. To stop the ritual now would be to bring terrible pain and disgrace on Running Deer. He needed the warrior. She was only another captive. Running Deer could afford a three-horse loss.

The Indians sat patiently. Running Deer had chosen to extend the torture. He would keep her far enough away from the fire to be in agony for hours. Any closer and she would pass out from pressure inside her head. A delicate balance had to be maintained between the height of the head and the size and heat of the fire.

Gertrude turned slowly now as the heat and a small breeze stirred, but she remained centered over the flames.

The squaw attending the fire began a slow chant. A second woman took it up, then all the squaws began the chant. It was a sign that the one being punished was almost ready to become unconscious.

Suddenly the woman at the fire wailed, stood and heaped more dry wood on the fire, then she did a little dance around the fire. The body was not lowered anymore. The torture was over, Gertrude had lapsed into unconsciousness.

Now the ritual took a different turn. The heat increased. Soon the top of the doeskin robe flamed up and burned away in front until it fell to the ground. Her breasts were now reddened and singed by the burning garment.

As she spun slowly in the heat, Gertrude's head and shoulders turned black from the soot.

The fire leaped six inches higher, and the chanting increased in tempo.

Another five minutes and blood began to seep from Gertrude's ears and hiss as it hit the fire below.

Soon blood came from her nose as the pressure inside her skull built and built as her blood boiled.

The squaw by the fire could tell almost the exact instant when it would happen. She kept up her dance around the body, then stopped, stared a moment and continued. The next time she stopped she threw her hands toward the sky, and at the same instant, the head exploded with a loud popping nose and blood, brains and fragments of her skull splattered the area.

The sound was the signal for the Indians to leave. The braves went first, back to their tepees. Then the women and children left, filing silently past the corpse, still hanging upside down over the fire, now burning lower and which would soon go out.

By custom the punished body would hang for three days over the dead fire, a reminder to all who looked at it that the laws of the tribe must be obeyed, or the tribe would disintegrate and there would be no safety, no protection from the whites or the Pony Soldiers.

Priscilla walked past the corpse of the girl she had known briefly on the train, but her eyes were closed. She stumbled, opened her eyes and saw the still terrified black holes where Gertrude's eyes had once been. The dark sockets seemed to be accusing her of betrayal.

Priscilla sobbed as she ran to the tepee of the chief, threw herself on her pallet and would not get up the rest of the day.

CHAPTER ELEVEN

BARLOW PUT THE last shovel full of rocks and dirt on the grave and filled in around the rough cross he had made with wire and two branches. It was the best he could do.

Barlow had made no plans. In his line of work if often didn't pay to plan too far ahead. He pushed the shovel to one side and sat down, letting his racing heart quiet. Must have been Yates' heart that gave out. He had been getting dizzy spells and blacked out once or twice. Barlow was determined the same thing would not happen to him.

He stared at their small operation. Even working it alone he should be able to take say eight to ten ounces of dust a day. That would be about two hundred dollars a day. If the good sand lasted for two weeks he would have . . . what? He had never been good with figures in his head. Fourteen days at two hundred would be two thousand eight hundred dollars. Plenty.

Barlow decided then. He would work to the end of paydirt, or he would stop in two weeks, and take his gold and get back to San Francisco. Yeah, the city by the bay.

As a precaution he took another look at the jar of gold in his small hiding place. It was still there. Last night he had taken a piece of paper and drawn a crude map. It showed plainly where the diggings were, all based on Bear Lake and the big river that ran into it. This canyon was three valleys to the north of the big river. He put the map back in the jar, left the top loose so the moisture in the bottom of the jar would evaporate, and went back to the sluice.

He stared into the long trough and found gold pasted against each of the baffles.

His heart swelled as he saw it. He had made it! He had struck it rich once in his life, and now he had proved that was no accident because again he had found gold—this time in the middle of nowhere, and he had been the *first* to find it!

He looked up at the cliffs around him. There were a hundred places someone could spy on him. Another prospector, or the Utes. He had been worried about them at first. He was deep into their hunting grounds, and they were known to deal harshly with prospectors. But so far he hadn't seen a sign of an Indian. Barlow was smart enough to know that did not mean the Utes had missed him. They might be ignoring him, or waiting their time.

Barlow shook off the feeling and began cleaning out the gold from the now almost dry trough.

It was truly a labor of love, digging out that

damp gold dust and putting it in the jar. He wouldn't mind doing it all day long!

He had just finished and held the jar in his hands, when he looked up and saw two Ute braves standing twenty feet from him. One had his bow bent with an arrow aimed at Barlow. Slowly Barlow raised his hands. He just prayed the savages knew what that meant.

The second Ute approached him slowly. He saw that the white man did not have a gun on his hip. All white men had guns. The Indian tied Barlow's hands together with rawhide, then picked up the jar the white man had been holding.

The Ute laughed when he saw it was only squaw clay. He would take it and show the chief.

They found his horse, and a second mount. They put everything on board the second horse which they thought might be useful. From the small camp they packed the tent, an axe and other tools that Spotted Tail said they always should bring back. The Ute knew the axe was too long for a war axe, but he supposed the squaws could find some use for it.

Soon they began moving, the two Indians riding the horses, not pleased with the saddles, but bringing them back as Spotted Tail had instructed them. The captive walked behind them, a white man's rope tied around his neck and to the saddle horn. He was an old man so they could not ride fast.

They came to the winter camp from the north, through the trees, and as soon as they came to the edge of the tepees, they were surrounded by all the children and squaws in the camp.

The squaws poked the white man with sticks, and spat on him. The young boys followed the example of the squaws but their sticks were sharp and they punctured the old man's clothing and drew blood. The boys howled in glee.

By the time they had reached Spotted Tail's tepee, the chief was standing outside. His white squaw stared with concern from the opening.

Spotted Tail lifted his hand and everyone stopped talking and shouting.

The braves quickly reported that he was a miner, that he had found some squaw clay and they had brought it along. They gave the jar to Spotted Tail and he nodded. He motioned to his white squaw.

"Talk," he said in English. He had been trying to learn the white man's language.

Priscilla came forward, embarrassed now about having no covering for her breasts. She smiled at the old man with the white beard. He smiled too, but could only stare at her naked breasts.

"I'm Priscilla Patterson, if we ever get out of here. Who are you?"

"Barlow, Jim Barlow from San Francisco."

"A long way from home. You found gold?"

"Yep, little placer operation. Just getting started."

"We're both in big trouble, Mr. Barlow. Utes hate miners and prospectors. I don't think I can help you much."

She turned back to Spotted Tail, and used the three words he had learned, "white man" and "friend."

Spotted Tail shook his head.

"He is not a friend. He comes, and then a thousand like him will come and ruin our streams and cut the trees from our mountains."

Priscilla used all the sign language she could. Eventually she made Spotted Tail understand her. She told him the man was old with many summers. He should be sent away, out of the Ute hunting grounds. That would be punishment enough.

The chief understood, but flicked his hand at the captive. He was taken to a post buried in the middle of the area, and tied there with his hands over his head.

Priscilla asked Spotted Tail if she could go talk to the prisoner. He scowled but nodded.

A man sitting nearby guarding the prisoner was given a sign by the chief, who then went back into his tepee.

Priscilla walked down to the post and smiled. "I'm afraid these Indians aren't good hosts."

"You're a prisoner yourself."

"Yes, but I'm not in as much trouble as you are. I'm sorry. They just hate prospectors and miners. Is that your gold?"

The chief had given him back his jar filled with dust.

"About the size of it. Not much to get killed for, is it?"

"They won't kill you."

"Like they didn't boil that woman's brains

128

out down there? I seen it done before. Made me watch once, then rousted me off their land. I hadn't taken any gold there. Wasn't any. Here, I won't be so lucky. They don't want anyone coming in here." He shook his head. "I'm in a hell of a fix this time." He scowled, then looked up. "Can you talk him into letting me go?"

"I didn't do much good trying to get myself free." She sighed and shook her head. "Why is it when everything seems to be going so right, that the whole world falls in on you?"

"Just like, I reckon, Miss. Nobody said it would be fair, just that it would be tough."

"How can we get you back to San Francisco?"

"Or even back to Salt Lake City, or Ogden?" he added.

"I don't imagine that you run too well. I would have tried to escape but I can't outrun the braves."

"I might hide from them, if I had a head start."

"I've heard they like to play hide and seek. The only trouble is you're *it* and when they find you, they use you for target practice."

"It's a chance, girl! Better than boiling my brains out, or getting scalped for practice."

"I'll try with the chief." She stopped. "The odds aren't good that you can outwit a tribe of Utes."

"Might be if we had some diversion. We could use a good army attack about now."

"That's too much to hope for. I've about given up on the army ever coming to find me."

That afternoon she spent two hours trying to

communicate with Spotted Tail about the old man. He was harmless. There wasn't enough gold in the hills to cause a gold rush. At last she said it would please her greatly if he would let the prospector go. It would make her think of Spotted Tail as a great chief.

She didn't know if he even understood all she tried to tell him. His face remained as stern and impassive as if he were sitting in the council.

After she had fixed his evening meal, and he had made love to her more gently than usual, he turned her face to him. "Tomorrow, round eye will run," he said. She stared at him. She had no idea he knew so much English.

Spotted Tail let a small smile touch his face. He turned over and went to sleep.

Run? What did he mean by that? The old miner would never be able to win a footrace. What did the chief mean? She thought of Barlow sitting against the post outside. By morning he might be so stiff and sore and stove up he couldn't even walk. But she dare not let him go. Then she would have to take his place. What kind of a deadly game did Chief Spotted Tail have in mind?

Morning came too quickly for Priscilla. She had slept in fits and starts, more worried about the old miner than she realized or understood. She had only met him yesterday.

Scouts reported to the chief every two hours, and he looked more and more grim. Mid morning everyone gathered at the center of the camp and the old miner was untied. The chief told Priscilla how the *game* would be played and she was to tell the miner.

He used his few English words and signs, and soon she understood. She shivered and then went to talk to Barlow.

Priscilla cried as she touched him. She couldn't keep the tears out of her eyes.

"I tried to get him to let you go, but he says you must run. The chief says he will give you your pistol and twenty rounds, and a headstart of two hundred yards. Then the chief will send twenty braves with bows and arrows to try to catch you. If you can kill one brave with each bullet, you will go free."

"Hot damn! Big chance. I might get a few, but not twenty. I don't run too good, no more."

"Like you said, at least it's a chance."

"Tell him I'll do it if he'll set one of the white girls free, turn her over to the army I hear is camped somewhere around here."

"I'll try." She talked to the chief who at last understood.

The chief smiled. This old man was soft like a woman. His braves would have no trouble with him. He shook his head at his own white squaw and she returned to the old man.

"He just shook his head," she said.

"At least you tried." Barlow looked at her. Maybe he should tell her where the gold mine was. No, she was a captive herself. Maybe the army was out there. They should be by now. He saw the chief coming and stood up straight and as tall as he could. The chief himself cut the bindings, handed him his pistol and a box of the right sized shells. There were no rounds in the cylinder. Smart old bastard, Barlow thought.

Twenty braves lined up across from him. All had bows and arrows, three in their hand and a pack on their back. It would be no contest. Barlow walked around in a small circle, took out six .44 rounds and held them in his hand. His legs came alive again. At least he could walk.

"Tell them I'm going to walk the first two hundred yards, after that they'll have to find me." He looked at the Chief. Spotted Tail nodded.

Barlow turned away from the open valley and walked toward the closest and thickest woods. There was no way to tell for sure when he had gone two hundred yards because he vanished into the thicket after the first fifty yards. The Indians looked at their chief. The chief looked at Priscilla.

She began counting, and the chief understood. When she got to one hundred and fifty, she nodded and the chief waved his men away.

"Good luck, Barlow," she said. It was more of a prayer than a goodbye.

Barlow began running as soon as he was out of sight. He went downhill, sticking to the hardest ground he could find. He angled toward a thick stand of pines, and climbed a small one, then got into a larger one and moved higher to a point where second growth tree tops crowded the old growth and could almost hide him. He broke off a branch and used it as a final shield, then he remained absolutely still.

It was almost five minutes later that the trackers came down his trail, lost it on the hard ground and the Indians fanned out, angry that they had lost the quarry so quickly. This was supposed to be live target hunting practice for them. Now they had to use all of their skills.

Six men ran ahead, watching for any sign of the round eye.

The trackers came on relentlessly. They had no tracks now, were taking directions and then crossing the routes of travel to try to find the telltale signs that the white man had passed that way.

Barlow's hand pressed the jar in his pocket that held the gold and the map. Then he made a conscious effort to freeze himself to the branch where he sat. His feet were on a branch just below and he was balanced well. The Utes would soon think to look upward and they would watch for anything out of the ordinary. They might even see where he broke off the pine bough.

Through the screening of pine needles he saw a runner racing to the searchers. He said something to the lead scout, who turned at once and ran back toward the camp. The messenger shouted something and all but two of the trackers turned and hurried away.

Barlow could not figure what had happened. The only thing he could think of that would cause such activity would be an impending attack on the camp, or an offensive strike. He watched the two remaining Utes below him. One left and made a large circle, trying to cut a trail. The other Indian worked around the trees, then the spot of shale rock, but nowhere could he find the trail continuing.

At last the tracker looked up. Barlow did not move. The tracker below drew his bow and before the miner could wince, the Ute fired an arrow into the cluster of tops next to the old growth pine. The arrow darted through the pine needles and sunk into the trunk of the pine a foot from Barlow's head. Another arrow bored through the pine needles higher, glanced off a limb and missed hitting the tree trunk.

When Barlow looked again, the tracker had left the ground and worked his way up the trunk of a small pine. He was coming up to check it out. He knew the quarry had to be close by. Now Barlow studied the area around him. He could not see or hear the Utes. Evidently all but these two had been called back to the Camp for some emergency.

One shot would kill this Ute, but it would bring the other back quickly. He had no other weapon. The Ute had left his bow on the ground. Barlow tried to figure a way out of this deadly trap. Then he realized he held it in his hand— the four foot long pine branch. The butt end was almost two inches thick. If he jammed it like a spear, he had a chance to knock the Indian off the limbs and disable him when he hit the ground. It was the best solution to his problem.

Barlow waited. The Indian worked quickly to

the old growth pine, then came hand over hand upward, pausing now and then to stare at the mass of pine branches.

The old miner was patient. He waited until the Ute was only three feet away and had drawn his knife. Then Barlow used his strong right arm and grasping the branch half way up thrust it downward at the Ute's chest as hard as he could. The Indian yelled in surprise and fear, then the branch smashed into his open mouth, jolted his head back and Barlow could hear the Indian's neck snap as it broke and he fell through the branches to the ground below.

Now it didn't matter what else happened. Barlow knew he had to get down from the tree and leave. He had no way to bury the Indian. He scrambled down, took the Indian's knife and bow and arrows and went deeper into the pine forest, climbing the side of the valley, and working downward. If there were something out there that had frightened the Indians, it could be a friendly force to him, maybe an army! He would be delighted to see a long column of Blue Coats right now!

Barlow ran when he could, then slowed, looked for hard ground and rested, then hurried on. When he had covered what he figured was five miles, he headed back downhill toward the valley floor.

He knew that when the second tracker found nothing, he would double back and start over again, and then he would find his dead partner and the fresh set of Barlow's tracks. So the Ute was somewhere behind him. He had to remember that, no matter what else happened, death was just behind him.

An hour later he came to a small rise just off the valley floor and looked downstream. Far below, maybe another three or four miles, he spotted a column of dust lifting into the still air.

Dust! That would be only from a mounted cavalry army patrol in force! There had to be at least a hundred horses to raise a dust trail like that! He would hurry toward them, and pray that he could hook up with the dust makers whoever they were, before his old legs gave out and the young legs of the Ute caught up with him and tried to lift his scalp.

He trudged on, each step now becoming a struggle. Once behind him he thought he had seen movement. If so, it could only be the Ute coming in. Faster! Another step. Another step. He had to keep moving. If he stopped, he died, it was that simple.

Another step down the valley, then one more. He threw away the bow and arrows, and it bouyed him for a while. He had to keep moving. There was no other way if he wanted to stay alive!

CHAPTER TWELVE

SPUR MCCOY ORDERED the hundred man army unit to break camp early that morning and march five miles west heading directly upstream toward Spotted Tail's winter camp. He knew the Utes had been watching the encampment. He wanted to be sure that they knew that he knew they were up there. It was the quickest way Spur could think of to force a parley. After a few hours in position, he would send out a three man party under a flag of truce. A three person party, since Istas must be one.

The move went with no problems. Spur had set out flankers and roving pickets and scouts well ahead of his party so there would be no surprises. He did not expect Spotted Tail with his thirty braves to attack a force he knew was composed of at least a hundred rifles.

From time to time the scouts reports that they had seen lone Ute warriors, riding hard away from the march.

As they rode, Istas had some new information for Spur.

"McCoy, I hope we can rescue the two Mormon girls, but I really don't think that the communities they come from will accept them back as full members of the Mormon society."

"Because they have lived with the Indians?"

"Yes, and because they are mature and without question have been used as sex slaves. There's a chance that Spotted Tail has kept the senator's daughter for himself. The chiefs sometimes pick out the prettiest one or the best worker and buy her from the brave who captured her."

"At least she's not Mormon. How can this church group be so narrow minded?"

"They are Mormon. It is a very strict and closed society. If you aren't in it, you almost have to leave town. It's that tight. If the local bishop says the stake is to deny the girls the welcome of the community, they will be shut out."

"Terrible! How can these people claim to be members of a church? It even has something of a Christian background."

"Since the girls have been sexually violated their bodies are no longer important. Now, only their souls will be cared for, and that has nothing to do with the body. To the church the two girls will be the same as dead."

"They seem like such normal people."

"In some ways they are. They're open and friendly, generous and giving."

The scout, Kirk rode up and reported. He sent a squirt of brown tobacco juice into the grass.

"The redskins are making way, moving back the way you expected. No contact with them, and not a shot fired."

"Good. I've told the men to keep it that way. How much farther to the five mile point?"

"Half a mile."

"Good."

As Spur watched the point trio of riders leading the group, he saw two of them spur forward, and the third turn and gallop toward the main body four hundred yards to the rear. Spur dug in his spurs and raced toward the retreating point man.

Jim Barlow saw the Pony Soldiers clearly now. Not more than a quarter of a mile away. Then he glanced behind and saw the Ute's head drop behind a log. Barlow had stuck to the edge of the timber for as long as he could. The Ute had shot two or three arrows at him, coming close each time but missing. Once Barlow was in the open the redman would have the advantage of open shots.

But the time had come. He pulled his left leg forward with his hand grasping his pants leg, then turned and fired a shot at the Indian who stood to shoot an arrow. Both shots missed, and Barlow staggered into the thick grass, moving toward the column of Pony Soldiers.

Barlow wanted to attract the soldier's attention. He fired two more shots at the Indian, then struggled forward. He got twenty yards away from the woods and an arrow slammed into his left leg. He screeched and tumbled into the grass. It wasn't quite tall enough to hide him.

The old miner lifted up, saw the brave

nocking another arrow. Barlow aimed deliberately and fired. He saw the round tear through the redman's leg and he went down. Barlow tried to stand. He broke the arrow off that protruded from his leg, and screamed. Tears welled up and spilled down his cheeks.

"Damned savages!" He lifted up on his good leg, swung up his left and stumbled forward. He saw the lead trio of soldiers pointing at him, then two rode forward and one to the rear. He turned and fired two more shots at the Indian. Then he reloaded his six-gun as he rested.

With five shots in place he lifted up and staggered another three steps toward the charging soldiers. He glanced back and saw the hostile raise his bow. Barlow turned and fired twice. He saw the bow release the arrow and knew he should be going down, diving into the grass, but when he tried, his wounded leg, snapped backward, locked in place and before he could surge in the other direction, the arrow struck him in the back.

Two hundred yards away, the corporal on the lead cavalry mount fired his rifle at the running Indian. He reloaded and fired again, this time hitting the Ute and dropping him. The Pony Soldier spurred his mount forward, raced past the downed white man and came toward the Ute in the grass. The Ute lunged upward and shot one arrow at the trooper. The arrowhead penetrated the edge of blue pants and dug into the saddle leather.

Corporal Callahan fired four times with his

pistol, killing the Ute. He swung around to check on the old man.

By the time the corporal got back to the downed man, Colonel McCoy and a trooper were there. The Colonel held the old man's head on his lap.

"Don't try to talk, Barlow. You're hurt bad. We'll get our trooper medical man up here to help." He nodded at the private who left, mounted and rode toward the main body.

"Too late for that," Barlow said. "Damn near made it. Oh, white girls in the injun camp. Three of them."

"Only three left?" Spur asked.

Barlow nodded. "Just three." He reached in his baggy pants and took out the jar. It glittered with gold dust. He handed it to Spur. "Take care of this for me. I don't make it, use it proper. Map inside there. Little placer operation. Damned Utes found us. Yates' heart give out on him." Barlow groaned and closed his eyes. Spur tried to ease the pressure of the arrow. It didn't help.

"Damn! One lousy arrow from making it. Guess that's the way it is. Not fair, just tough." He looked up at Spur. There was a relaxed kind of peace in his eyes. He smiled. Then he died.

The trooper turned away. Spur put down the old head in the grass, broke off the arrow and threw it away.

Captain Fowler had stopped the troop and formed the men up into a pair of company streets for the bivouac. They had the new, small ground covers that could be used as two-man tents. Now they would put them up in a smart row to show Spotted Tail that they were really an army, not a ragtag bunch of freebooters.

Spur stood and looked at the jar of gold dust, then down at the old prospector. Not even the threat of the Utes could keep him and his partner from a possible strike. Spur walked over and looked at the Ute Indian. He sent for a spare mount trailing the wagon and had the Ute tied across its back. Tomorrow when they talked, they would send the warrior back to his people.

Spur put the jar of gold inside his shirt. The story was out. Before he got back to the main body, every trooper in the unit knew about the gold, the dead prospector and the close by strike. Gold fever was always a problem for the army. A few lucky pans of sand could earn a deserter twice his army pay for the year.

Back in the rapidly forming camp, Spur showed the jar to Istas, who had taken over Lt. Windsong's tent, with a guard outside for her protection.

"Is that real gold dust?" she asked. "I've never seen any before."

"It's real," Spur said as he slumped in the officer's camp chair. "And it's bound to cause us some problems."

"There's a paper," Istas said, digging into the top of the jar with a finger. She took out the piece of paper, tapped off the gold powder into the jar and unfolded the paper.

Spur looked at it over her shoulder.

"Not much of a map. It shows Bear Lake, then the big river where we are and three small streams to the west. On the third stream is a spot marked with an X."

"Can't be too hard to find a placer mine with a sluice box," Istas said.

"But let's hope no one tries to find it," Spur said. "It can only mean trouble." He put the map back in the jar and pushed it inside his shirt.

Spur went outside and watched the camp forming up. Two men returned with a four point buck deer that had shot a short way into the hills. There would be fresh venison for everyone that night at supper.

Spur watched the developments and received word every two hours from his scouts and pickets. The Indians were not moving. Everything was quiet. The army would send out its negotiating team in the morning.

Lt. Windsong had been relegated to a small tent just up from the captain's in officer country, and he sat there pondering. Sgt. Bennedict was out of the question. He was too loyal to the captain. But there would be another man. He would select one and simply order him and it would be done. The sergeant selected wouldn't know he was going on a raid until it was too late.

"Yes!" Windsong said out loud. He looked around but no one had heard him. He would take twenty men, two squads. And he would do it as soon as it was dark, while the colonel and captain were still having their wine. Yes! They would be away and into enemy territory before Landower could mount a force to come after him.

"Then the heathen red savages will pay for putting a blemish on my career!" Lt. Windsong said softly. He said the same words over and over again.

When his tray of roast venison came slightly before dark, Lt. Windsong was so keyed up he couldn't eat. He put the tray down and as dusk fell, he walked along the row of small tents until he found Sgt. Anderson. He called the sergeant aside.

"Sgt. Anderson, you've been picked to go with me on a special patrol. This new colonel wants to be sure the Utes don't sneak out of their camp tonight and get away. I want you to bring two squads of ten men each. Tell no one where you're going or what you are doing. This must be done quickly and quietly. We don't want the Utes to hear us coming. Each man should have his usual issue of combat ammunition, a hundred and twenty rounds for his rifle and fifty for his pistol. You have five minutes, Sergeant, to get the men to the horses. And remember, quietly. The other troopers must not know where we are going."

The sergeant saluted and hurried away. Lt. Windsong strolled to the line where the horses had been staked out, had a trooper saddle his mount and waited.

Within a minute or two troopers began drifting in, saddling up and moving quietly out into the darkness a hundred yards from the camp.

Ten minutes later the troops were ready, Lt. Windsong gave the order and they moved out at a walk toward the winter camp.

"Sergeant, be sure every man's rifle and pistol are loaded. No one should fire until I give the command."

"Yes sir." The word was passed.

Lt. Windsong led the troopers up the broad valley, staying to the left hand side where it was the most open. Two miles up the valley, the moon went under scudding clouds and they swung closer to the darkness of the pine and brush woodlands.

An owl hooted to the north. They proceeded at a walk through the darkness.

An owl hooted slightly behind them.

They were forced closer to the woods by a small stand of timber in the valley. It was the obvious route and Lt. Windsong did not hesitate. His twenty men had formed into a column of twos and were spaced out at five yard intervals. As the front of the column entered the narrower area, a hail of arrows slammed into men, horses and trees.

One trooper took an arrow through both cheeks. He broke it off and screamed, jolting off his mount which also was hit and fled in terror.

Horses and Pony Soldiers all around him had been hit by the arrows, now a blinding barrage of rifle fire came at the soldiers from both sides. Indians had lain in wait in the island of timber and now both fired at an angle northward so they would not hit their own men in the deeper woods.

"Retreat! Fall back!" Sgt. Anderson bellowed. He was one of the few still mounted. He spurred for the rear, met more fire but escaped it and rode out of the heaviest hail of lead.

He tied his horse and ran back, helping wounded men as they staggered to the rear. He caught four horses, and tied them near his. Soon he had six troopers with rifles, and he put them in a line and ordered them to fire into the woods where the enemy shots had been launched.

They fired a dozen rounds each, then Sgt. Anderson called a cease fire. The enemy fire had stopped.

He heard an owl hoot from far up the valley.

"They've gone," he whispered to a trooper. "Let's move back in there and see what we can salvage. They all can't be dead."

It was a gruesome quest. The first ten yards they found three dead troopers. Another man had an arrow through his thigh and screamed until he passed out. They carried him back to the horses. They caught four more mounts, two of which were wounded. At the head of the column they found Lt. Windsong. He had been wounded slightly in the arm and had been pinned under his dead mount. They rolled the black off him and he stood, dazed, but not seriously hurt.

Ten minutes later a squad of troopers rode in from the main camp led by Sgt. Bennedict. Each carried a kerosine lantern and went to work bandaging up the wounded, catching horses and laying out the dead.

Lt. Windsong had found a horse and mounted up. He sat there with a bandage on his arm, above all of it, seemingly remote from the death around him.

A corporal from the camp reported to Sgt. Bennedict.

"We have ten dead and six wounded. We've found twelve horses. The rest have scattered. We won't catch them until morning."

"Very well, Corporal. I'm leaving you here with six men to protect the dead. Start two fires to let the Utes know you're here, but stay out of the firelight. We'll transport the wounded back to camp, and send out another dozen men to reinforce you. Be careful."

They got the walking wounded on horses but had to leave one man with the dead until they could bring a wagon for him. He had been crushed by a falling horse. Chances were he would die if they moved him. The chances were also high that he would be dead by morning if they left him there.

When Sgt. Bennedict reported to Captain Landower a half hour later, the red-haired career cavalry officer's face turned as red as his hair.

"Lt. Windsong was on that fool's mission?"

"Yes sir, commanded it from what Sgt. Anderson told me. The sergeant is right outside, sir, he wasn't wounded."

"Bring him in."

Sgt. Anderson came into the tent and stood stiffly at attention.

"Relax, Sergeant, I have a few questions."

The trooper unbent a little.

"Did you have orders to take out twenty men?"

"Yes, sir."

"Who gave the orders?"

"Lt. Windsong, sir. I just guessed they came from you."

"They did not. The patrol was not authorized."

"I was obeying orders of a commissioned officer."

"No blame on you, Sergeant. You acted properly. Did Lt. Windsong give you a reason for the trip?"

"Yes sir. He said the colonel was afraid the Indians might sneak out of the camp during the night."

"A reasonable explanation. See to your men." He turned to Bennedict. "Have you sent out relief for the guards at the site?"

Sgt. Bennedict said he had, ten more men.

Captain Landower scowled. "Yes, good, Bennedict. We'll get the rest of this straightened out in the morning." He swore Sgt. Bennedict to secrecy and told the sergeant to guard Lt. Windsong while the officer dug graves for the ten men who died.

"Christ!" Captain Landower shouted when the sergeants left. Now he knew that he should have executed Lieutenant Windsong two weeks ago and had it over with. Windsong seemed determined to ruin the captain's army career one way or the other.

Spur McCoy had sat in the corner of the tent watching the interviews. He shook his head at the mess one stupid army officer could make of things. Lt. Windsong was going down, sooner or later, and Spur would put Capt. Landower in for a medal. He would make sure that this popinjay did not ruin the captain's career.

CHAPTER THIRTEEN

IT WAS NEARLY ten P.M. when Spur roused Istas from her sleep. She sat up, topless, and smiled at him.

"One last try to get one or two of the girls out of the winter camp before our parley," Spur said. "We need all of the advantages we can get. Do you mind taking a ten mile ride in the moonlight?"

"Not with you." She reached out and kissed him, hugged him tightly and Spur was tempted to put off the ride. He grinned and pulled away from her.

"Later for that sexy girl stuff. You want to get some clothes on so the guards don't go crazy?"

"Yes. I hope we can save at least one of the girls," she said. "One of them must have been killed somehow from what the old miner said." She slipped into her pants and shirt, and took her squaw dress with her. They went into the darkness and toward the horses.

Spur talked to the guard, told him where they were going, saying that if they didn't show up by daylight, the guard should tell the captain.

They saddled three horses, and Spur led one as they rode west up the broad valley.

Well before they came to the site of the ambush, where two big fires burned brightly, they cut into the timber, circled to the south and planned to come up on the southern side of the winter camp.

The going was slow through the trees and brush. Spur missed one valley and they had to back track half a mile. It was just before midnight when they left their horses and moved up to the deep woods near camp. Spur told her to watch for sentries, and they spent another hour moving up to the camp. They saw two lookouts, but went around both easily.

Now they lay on the grass at the edge of the woods staring at the tepees.

They had talked about it. One of the girls was with the chief. It would not be realistic to try to get her. They would go for one of the others. Istas remembered where she had seen a white girl before, and they concentrated on that tepee. If she was the girl who had died, they would try to find out where the other captive was.

Istas came out of the brush in her buckskin robe and walked directly to the target tepee. It was not the closest to the woods, but backed up toward the council fire area. Istas had a sharp knife with her and when she reached the tepee, she cut a two-foot slice in the heavy skins and wedged inside.

Spur was moving toward the spot before he heard anything, and before she reappeared. By the time he got there he saw a brave leave another tepee and fade into the night in the other direction. Spur lifted and spread the sides of the slit. He met a brown-eyed face coming out. The eyes were sleepy, but her skin was white, tanned now from all her outside exposure, but there was an excited look in her eyes and a not-really-believing-it expression. Spur took her hand and helped her out, then they ran silently for the woods.

At every step he expected a rifle to fire, but none did. He looked back and saw Istas struggling with a squaw. Istas flashed the knife and the squaw took a step back, then charged. Istas tripped her, dropped with her knee on the woman's throat and whispered something to her.

At once Istas was up and running toward the woods. The squaw shrieked at the back of the tepee. She screamed and screamed, waking up the camp. But by the time the braves came running, she could only say that one of the white girls was gone.

Spur and the girl ran hard through the woods to the horses. They didn't wait for Istas. Spur did not worry about her finding her way out. They found the horses. He helped the white girl mount and they rode hard. When they came to the point where the lookout had been, the post had been moved and they rode through as fast as they dared.

Spur cut back through the trees toward the valley as soon as he was a mile downstream.

When they came out on the grassy valley, they found Istas waiting for them.

"Slowpokes," she said, teasing them. Then they rode hard for a half mile and walked the horses for half a mile. They jogged on toward the twin fires they saw ahead. They made a wide circle around the soldiers' fires.

The girl was one of the Mormons and she would not talk about what had happened to her friend. She said her name was Bessie.

"It's too horrible," she said. "The squaws made me watch the whole thing."

They assured her that she was safe now, and that soon she would be back with her family in Ogden.

"They won't take me," the girl said defiantly.

"They better," Spur said. "If your father won't take you in as his daughter, I'll pound him into a pulp and twist his arm until he agrees."

Bessie began to cry, and Istas rode alongside and then stopped and held her in her arms.

When her sobbing stopped they moved again.

"Even if they do take me back, they'll just marry me off quickly to somebody as a second or third wife. I'll never really have a life of my own."

"You will, Bessie, you will," Spur said suddenly angry with a man he didn't even know, or have any reason to resent. "I can promise," he said. For some reason he kept thinking about the jar of gold dust, the placer mine map and the last words of the old miner to use the gold *proper*.

They slipped back into camp, Bessie bunking down with Istas and Spur taking to his blankets on the floor inside the captain's tent. He and the captain had entered into a lively discussion about sleeping accomodations. Spur asked the captain when he last had slept on the ground. The captain couldn't remember. Spur urged him to stay on his folding cot, while he took another blanket for a mattress and stretched out on the ground.

When morning arrived, Spur had already brought a spare uniform to Istas's tent. It was the smallest that the quartermaster had. Istas could cut and shorten the pants, and soon Bessie would have some more suitable clothes. She had been wearing only an old skirt when they rescued her. Spur decided something a little less revealing would help.

Captain Landower heard about his mission before Spur got back to the tent for breakfast.

"So you got one! Well done. I just wish it had been the senator's niece. Would have been so much better."

"We'll get her today. I plan to move out with the parley team at ten this morning."

"And where do you want the troops?"

"I want sixty of you with rifles held with their butts on the saddles so Spotted Tail can see them. You'll back us at a hundred yards. I'll also need six horses, unsaddled, with rope bridles."

"You wouldn't. It's not at all according to regulations."

"I don't hold much to regulations when I'm

154

dealing with human lives, especially female lives."

Captain Landower scowled. "Damnit, you're right, of course. I've been out here in the bloody sun too long. You can have ten horses to buy back each girl with if you want them. Damn! I don't know what I'm thinking about."

Spur smiled. "I do. Windsong. Not the crazy, inept, dunderhead of a lieutenant, but his sharp, political powerful general class officer father. You're thinking that if Lt. Windsong had been one of those killed last night, that General Windsong would have hounded you right out of the army. Right?"

"Right. You know he could do it."

"Not anymore. I've got some influence in Washington. I know a few senators, about thirty I'd say by name, and they know me and my family. Then too, I work directly with the President. When I get back to St. Louis, I'll send off a batch of reports to the army, to the President, to my boss and to every senator who votes on the appropriations for the army. There will be no hatchet job done on you by Windsong. If he tries, I'll do my best to get him thown out of the army!"

Captain Landower smiled for the first time in two days. He looked at Spur and shook his head.

"I . . . I really don't know what to say. Lt. Windsong has been such a pain in the ass."

"I've met him," Spur said and both men laughed. After that Captain Landower ate a good breakfast and was in fine spirits as he called his top noncoms in for a briefing.

* * *

The night before when Spur and Istas stole the white girl out from under his doubled guards, Spotted Tail realized his tribe was at a serious crossroads. He was afraid of the Pony Soldiers. He knew what they could do with their thousand rifles and ten thousand bullets. It was smart to be afraid of something that could kill you.

He paced inside his tepee, woke his white squaw and told her to go back to sleep, then went outside and walked in the moonlight.

What he feared most was a dawn raid on his village and a massacre of his tribe. It had happened before by the Blue Coats with other Indian tribes.

He made a decision and called a brave to wake all the women and children. They would go higher into the hills to the old summer and berry picking camp. The women and children would stay there for two days and then they would be told what to do. They should take enough food with them for two days.

He had decided that the white squaw would stay at the winter camp. He didn't think the Pony Soldiers could have stolen the white squaw, but he had no idea who did. They wanted the two white squaws. He would keep them at this camp, so they would not endanger the Indian women and children.

It was early in the morning when the women had gone. They would have to walk most of the night, but that was routine for them.

156

He woke up Priscilla, stroked her soft white breasts and told her what he had done.

"The army is here and they want to take us back?" she asked. He was understanding more and more English. He nodded. "Will you fight with the army?"

Spotted Tail shook his head. "A thousand rifles," he said.

She smiled. Indians had little understanding of numbers over ten. "Will they come tomorrow?"

"Tomorrow or the next day."

"Then we shouldn't waste time. Show me what an Indian bride must do on her honeymoon."

Spotted Tail laughed. He stripped the soft fabric from her body, kissed her breasts and said he would be right back. He went outside to make sure that his lookouts had been posted. The minute the army broke camp or moved a sizable group of men toward him, he wanted to know about it.

The chief went back to his tepee, closed the flap and pulled off the few clothes he wore. She caught him while he was standing up. She put her arms around his neck, then jumped up and wrapped her legs around his torso. She had seen his cock was stiff and ready.

"Like this, standing up," she said. He frowned not understanding. She let go with one hand and reached between them, found his stiff phallus and moved slightly to make the connection, then she pushed herself forward, impaling his shaft inside her.

Chief Spotted Tail laughed at first, then as she ground herself against him, and worked back and forth he began to get excited. Soon he was pumping his hips at her faster and faster.

He shouted, then shouted again, as he climaxed. Then he knelt down, still holding her, still fastened firmly to her and lay on his back on the pallet. He held her tenderly and spoke to her in his own language so he could say exactly what he meant.

"Small, white squaw, you have been a delight to my old age. You have turned the fall of my years into a joy and excitement that is remarkable. I will remember you always. But there is not the possibility that I can stand up against so many Blue Coats. If we run away, they will follow us. They will wound and kill my women and children as well as my braves. There is nothing else I can do. We are a sparse people. There are fewer of us left than the eagles that fly in the sky. I cannot let my people be slaughtered for what to us is legal and just, but to the round eye is evil and unlawful."

He stopped and she reached in and kissed his lips. She seemed to enjoy doing that. He lifted her forward and lowered her breasts into his mouth to chew on them. It aroused him again, but he waited. She tired of his ministrations and lifted up and sat on him and stared down.

"Chief Spotted Tail. I'm not sure what all that was you said, and you won't understand much of this, but I want to say it. I know the army is out there, and that they may come tomorrow or the next day. I just pray to God that you don't fight with them about me and the other white girl. No one or two people are important enough that others should die because of them.

"The people I know in Washington and back in Pennsylvania will never believe me when I tell them about all this. Well, some of them will believe it. I'm not even sure how old you are, forty, forty-five, maybe even fifty. But you make love like a young man. You're the best lover I've ever had. Really. And I have known what, twenty, maybe twenty-five different lovers. You are the best!" She slid off him and lay beside him.

Without a word he moved over her again, lowered and entered her and she cried out in joy and delight and they made it last for an hour, both coming near to their peaks, then stopping, making it last and last and last, until finally neither could hold back any longer and they climaxed together in a long shouting, wailing union that sheened their bodies with sweat, and set one of the dogs outside to wailing.

They collapsed on the pallet in each other's arms, and it was the way they went to sleep.

Only the barking dogs woke them in the night. They felt for each other, and made love again, quickly this time, sharply, hard pulsing and driving and with a peaking of emotions so strong that they both cried a little. Then Spotted Tail touched her lips with his fingers and rolled away from her. He pulled on his loin cloth, his leggings and moccasins and put on the faded shirt that he had stolen somewhere, then he went into the darkness.

She sat there, wondering if she would ever see him again.

Priscilla Patterson sat up and hugged her knees to her chest. Yes, she would see him again, but never this way. He was gone now to be ready when the soldiers came. They would have a talk, she hoped. It was always so much better to talk than to fight.

She thought of the Ute Indian chief, darker than many Indians, and the way he had treated her and honored her among his wives, and the way he had loved her. She would never forget him, never, no matter what the next few hours and days held.

She would never forget him.

CHAPTER FOURTEEN

LT. WINDSONG SAT on his footlocker in the shade of a tree. He had bribed two enlisted men to move the box. He was feeling better. He remembered the abortive attack last night. Everything had been against him. The damned Indians had ambushed him. It could have happened to anyone. Now they blamed him.

He touched his wounded arm. They had put some ointment on it and wrapped it with a cloth. If they had a doctor along he would have had some real treatment.

He blinked back tears. He had cried once already this morning. What had gone wrong? It seemed like such a good idea his father had to send him West to an outpost where he could get some Indian fighting experience. His father had told him that to rise in the ranks he would need to be bloodied against the Indians. They had carefully selected Camp Pilot Butte in Wyoming as one of the most peaceful and benign of the army posts in Indian country. Somehow it had not worked out.

He stared at the handcuffs. He would trade the five hundred dollars in his footlocker to be rid of those blasted manicles! He had no idea what he was going to do, but he had to do something before the army courtmartialed him and sent him to a federal prison in chains.

Do something!

Slowly his mind recalled the events of the past three or four days. First the attack on his group posting pickets, then this abortive thrust last night. He took a short stick and pounded it a dozen times into the ground. Think! He had never had any trouble coming up with new plans.

Attack the Utes! Charge the bastards in their winter camp. Take revenge for them ruining his army career. Attack! Attack! Attack!

But how? He was manacled to the damn foot locker!

Money! It always worked. He had over forty dollars right now in his pocket. Three months wages for most of the enlisted men.

Sgt. Bennedict walked by and looked at him. Lt. Windsong turned away. The bastard! There was one man Windsong could kill without a moment's regret. The fucking bastard! He talked his head off about that first attack, and last night, too.

Curiously, Bennedict turned and walked back, this time directly toward him. As he came he slipped a flask from his pocket.

He grinned as he stopped six feet away.

"Well, the great Lt. Windsong has been nailed to the ground. Not any fun is it, Windsong?" He held up his hands. "Hey, don't get all mad and red-faced. I know you don't like me, and you're not one of my best buddies either. But right now, we need each other."

"Get out of my sight, you pile of shit! I don't need you!"

Sgt. Bennedict laughed. "You just don't know. How long has it been since you've had a shot of whiskey? I've got nearly a pint right here in my hand. You interested?"

Windsong reached out but it was too far away.

"I'd say you're interested. I give you the flask, and fill it up for you again, and we talk, we bargain. All right?"

Windsong was licking his lips. He nodded. He would talk with anyone for a drink.

The enlisted man passed the flask and Windsong bent and took a drag from it and sighed in appreciation. Then he hid the flask under his shirt and looked back at the enlisted man.

"Now, what do you want?"

"Not much, Windsong, it's what you want that's important. I can get you out of those cuffs, on a horse and a chance to attack the Utes. A chance to get back at the bastards who ambushed you last night."

Windsong sat up straighter, his brain working at top speed. How could a sergeant do it? Yes, he could. His men did what he told them. That was army. A chance to get back at the Utes!

His hand trembled as he took anther drink. What he wouldn't give to get a crack at the Utes one more time! Attack!

"You help me?" Lt. Windsong asked.

"Hell yes, why not? Men have to help each other. Besides, I've got a good idea going."

"How many men could you get me?"

"That might be a problem. I hear there's going to be a parley this morning. Most of the men will be up there somewhere, or getting ready to go. I figure you get away first, and surprise everyone."

"Yes! I could be the first wave smashing into the Ute defenders. And they wouldn't have the darkness to hide in! I could get a clear shot at the bastards who cut down my men last night!" He took two more drags on the flask. He was feeling better. The booze was doing its work. He could whip ten men! Yes, let him go after those short, stupid little Utes! He would tear them to pieces!

He looked quickly back at the enlisted men. The troopers could not be trusted. They always were double-talking, double-dealing. Always. That's why they were only enlisted men. If they were honest and trustworthy and superior, they would be officers. He tipped the flask again. It was empty. He handed it back to the sergeant who gave him another one that was full.

The lieutenant grinned and slipped it inside his shirt. He stood and walked around the wooden footlocker he was chained to.

"You must want something from me. What?" A cunning smile came to Windsong's face. He was good at bargaining. He would wheedle this dumb enlisted man down to nothing.

"Almost nothing. What I want from you is

164

nothing compared to your grand attack on the Utes. I almost wish I could be with you!"

"Yes, it will be grand. It will be a slashing attack that men will remember, that women will write songs about, that they will study at West Point!" He frowned. "Now, what do you require of me?"

Sgt. Bennedict smiled. "Like I said. Almost nothing. You know about the jar of gold the old miner had?"

"Yes. I figured there was about twenty ounces there. Maybe four hundred dollars worth."

"All I ask of you, Lt. Windsong, sir, is that you get that jar for me from the colonel's quarters. He's staying in the captain's tent, and I can't get inside."

Windsong grinned, a cunning smile bathed his face. "So you want me to steal something from the colonel? You must be mad!" He took a pull from the new pint of whiskey, lowered it, shivered slightly, then took one more draw from it. He shook his head. "Why do you want the gold?"

"Hell, it's three years pay for me. Besides there is a map inside the jar."

Lt. Windsong tipped the pint again. It was good whiskey, at least by now it tasted good. But he knew his tongue was getting a little dulled to the taste. Get the jar. Hell, easy, bluff past the outside guard . . . he was an officer, take the jar and give it to the stupid sergeant. It would be found and returned, and the sergeant courtmartialed. Yes! That would be a sweet revenge for all the hell this man had caused him. He looked slyly at the sergeant.

"And when would I do this, get the jar of gold?"

"Right now. The colonel is out with the troops getting ready for a march. The captain is running a small patrol just to be sure there is no force of Indians on the ridge. The camp will be deserted in another half hour, and by then I'll have the gold, and you'll be on your way around the slow moving column, and charging in on the Utes."

"Yes, I'll do it!" Windsong said, making up his mind suddenly. They taught him at West Point that an officer had to make decisions quickly, do something, move, get into action.

Sgt. Bennedict sat down beside the officer, and took a powerful pair of metal cutters from his big pocket. He extended the handles and quickly cut the chain that held one manacle to the footlocker. Lt. Windsong was free. Only the one manacle circled his left wrist.

"Pull your shirt down over the iron, and the guard on the tent will never known. I'll meet you here near the captain's tent with a horse, outfitted with two rifles and two pistols so you can lead all the men I can bring with you."

Lt. Windsong nodded, stood and walked directly to the captain's tent. He tipped the flask once more, nearly draining it, wiped his lips and strode up to the trooper on duty outside the tent.

"Soldier, Captain Landower needs something from his quarters, he sent me for it." The lieutenant didn't pause. He saw the trooper salute as he walked by into the tent. The jar of gold sat on a rolled up blanket. It was in plain sight. He picked it up, made sure it was the gold jar, slipped it inside his shirt and strode out of the tent and toward the edge of the woods to the rear. It might be good for him to get out of sight until Sgt. Bennedict came with his horse and his troops.

He stepped into some bush and waited. As he leaned against a pine tree, he drained the last of the whiskey. His eyes blurred for a moment, then came back. He would do it! He would lead even ten men on a lightning raid and get the senator's niece back. She was the important one. He would bring her out riding in front of him on the saddle, and he would have to hold her and one of his hands would close around her snowy white breast and she would look back and nod and urge him to pet her more. Maybe they would stop on the way back and she would lift her skirts and let him see her milky white thighs and then her love nest and they would come together and make love all afternoon!

He shook his head as his eyes went fuzzy again. Then they cleared and he started to move from one tree to the next, but he stumbled and almost fell. Damn root, he must have caught his foot. He swore at the root, then looked up.

Sgt. Bennedict wasn't there yet. He wished he had some more whiskey. He would have all he wanted soon. He thought of how life had been in Omaha with his father. It was different at headquarters. Everything was theory and guesswork. Out here if you made a wrong decision it could cost you your life!

He was a garrison soldier, and after this was over his father would be able to keep him in administration somewhere. His duty out here would help, just like his daddy said.

Someone was coming! He shook his head to clear it, and then stared out at the camp. A rider, a lone rider. He was looking at the captain's tent, then moved out and rode the fringe of the woods. Slowly the man's face came into sharp focus, it was Sgt. Bennedict.

"Here!" Lt. Windsong called, and the horseman turned and rode into the woods. He swung down and handed the reins to the officer.

"Here we are, just as promised. Get the jar?"

"Yes." Lt. Windsong handed him the jar. The sergeant shook it from side to side, then opened it and pushed his finger into the gold dust and moved it around until he found a paper. He nodded and seemed to relax.

"All right, Lt. Windsong. The bargain is complete. I have ten men waiting for you in the edge of the woods a mile out of camp. They will be in the left hand timber and will come out to meet you when you ride in. My suggestion is that you ride now. Circle camp in the woods, and stay in the fringes until you meet the ten men. Then you'll need to swing wide to the south to miss the Indian scouts and come in on the unprotected flank."

"Sergeant! I don't need some mealy mouthed, low-born damned enlisted man to tell me tactics! I know how to soldier. Now get the hell out of here. I've got a fight ahead of me."

Windsong tried to get in the saddle twice. Then Sgt. Bennedict moved in and lifted his foot to the stirrup, and helped boost him into the leather. The officer almost fell off the other side, then steadied and sat firmly in the saddle.

"All right! I'm set. Get out of here!" The officer waited as Sgt. Bennedict pushed the jar of gold inside his shirt and ran back to his tent in the long line of enlisted men's low shelters.

Lt. Windsong squared his shoulders. A ten-man command, not bad. It would have to do. He blinked and then rode ahead, letting the horse find the way through the trees and brush. He would circle the camp, find his ten men and ride hard straight up the valley. No one would be able to stop him, not in daylight, when the filthy heathens had no place to hide!

He almost fell off his horse once, then held on tighter as it worked along the edge of the valley. When he was a mile past the end of camp he began looking for his troops.

They had to be here somewhere, they had been sent by Sgt. Bennedict. For a moment he thought he saw some troops ahead, then they were gone. He shook his head and rode to the spot. He was beyond the point where the ambush had taken place. He was heading in the right direction. But where were his troops?

He patted his guns. He had four troopers right here!

He could lead them into the fray!

Lt. Windsong sat on his horse and thought about it. No, he needed support. He must have the ten men. His eyes glazed thinking about the medal he would win. He turned and saw troopers riding up behind him. They said nothing, just ranged in a column of twos behind him and he motioned ahead. They rode erectly, with none of the usual chatter. They were all armed, but none of them looked familiar. Hell, no officer could know all of his men.

He led them into the valley and picked up the pace to a canter. The men followed in perfect discipline. See! Real cavalry troopers knew how to follow a true cavalry officer! Blood always made a difference. Breeding! That was the difference between the common trooper and the officers.

For a moment he looked behind him and he saw no one. His blood chilled, and then they were there again, their mounts now showing sweat and the men's faces glowing.

He rode on.

A mile later a whoop came from the side and a lone Ute warrior rode down from the woods, waved his bow and arrow at Lt. Windsong and vanished into the woods before the officer could get off a shot.

The officer looked behind him. None of his men had pulled their guns.

He looked over his shoulder, saw a corporal leading the men and screamed at him.

"The next time one of them attacks us, I want you to take three men and ride him down. Do you hear me, Corporal?"

All ten men behind him shouted in chorus, "Yes, Sir, Lt. Windsong!"

He smiled. They were getting the idea. He'd whip this batch of misfits into soldiers yet!

Another half mile down the valley, and still six miles from the camp, another Indian scout came charging out. Windsong fired twice at him with a pistol, missed and barely evaded three arrows the scout had fired.

He turned quickly. There was no one behind him. For a moment his mind froze, and then he shook his head and the ten troopers came back into focus and he saw them firing rifles at the hard riding Ute savage.

He heard return fire. Two of his men screamed and fell from their mounts behind him. The horses they had been riding remained in the formation. Unusual.

But Lt. Windsong had no chance to wonder about it. Ahead he saw a band of six Utes riding to meet him. He leveled his rifle and fired and loaded and fired at the Utes. He saw one go down, then he gave the order for his riders to spread out on either side of him in a charge formation. The men moved, and even the riderless horses swung into line. He could see the men firing their rifles from horseback. The two groups surged together.

Lt. Windsong felt a rifle ball whistle past him, and then something slammed into his shoulder and knocked him off his horse. He fell heavily, jolting his wounded arm and causing great pain in one leg as he hit the grassland and rolled. He still had his two pistols.

Quickly he looked around him and he saw only the Utes who circled him, shooting now and then, laughing at him.

Where were his men?

Then he saw them. The ten black army mounts circled the Utes on the outside, only the men riding them had no uniforms, they had no bodies! Each horse was sat by a skeleton with an army blue shirt on and on the brow, a low crowned campaign hat. They were all ghosts of men who had been killed under his command!

Lt. Windsong forgot about the ghostriders. He fired his pistols at the surging Utes. Some stayed just out of pistol range. Two dismounted, used army rifles and fired close to him but did not hit him. They waited for him to use up his ammunition.

After ten minutes the Indian riflemen both fired at once, and he felt his right arm flung to the side and the pistol sail into the air away from him. His arm had been hit near the elbow.

The Utes waited. When he raised up a little a rifle round dug through his left shoulder. He screamed.

It wasn't supposed to be this way!

Sgt. Bennedict would have the last laugh! The sergeant had tricked him. There were no ten men waiting for him. The sergeant wanted only to use him to get the gold jar, and then helped him go charging out on an idiot's mission!

Now he was going to die.

There was no doubt about that, the only question was when and how. He slowly reloaded one of his guns with his throbbing left hand. Six more bullets in his belt. Then . . .

He stared over the grass at his executioners. They were small men, darker than most Indians, and total savages. No wonder the white men were beating them back, stealing their land. They were not worthy to hold it!

A bullet from an army rifle now owned by a proud Ute, dug a jagged path through his right lung, and Lt. Windsong fell backward and lay looking up at the sun.

What had happened to all of his dreams?

Where had his plans gone?

What had happened to put him in a deadly situation like this?

There were a hundred more questions, all unanswered as an Indian knife slashed through the veins and tendons of his left wrist and the six-gun fell from his grasp.

Lt. Joseph Windsong stared at his bleeding wrist, then at the ugly, furious, painted face of terror that loomed over him, as the knife swung again and his neck from one side to the other burst forth with gushing, spurting blood.

Twenty seconds later Lt. Windsong ceased to exist.

CHAPTER FIFTEEN

SGT. BENNEDICT SALUTED smartly as he reported to the captain as the parley details was forming up.

"The Captain wanted to see me, sir?"

"Yes, Bennedict. Thanks for volunteering to stay as non-com in charge here while we move out to the parley. As you know, Lt. Windsong has left camp. I'm listing him as a deserter unless we find him up the valley somewhere. He was clearly out of his head the last time I talked with him."

"Yes, sir. I'll take care of things here."

Captain Landower looked at the sergeant sternly. "Good. I also have a report that you were talking to the lieutenant this morning. How did he seem to you when you talked?"

"Out of his head is the best way to describe him, sir. He asked me to get a horse for him. He pleaded with me to unlock the manacles. He was screaming at me most of the time. I left as soon as I could get away from him."

"He said nothing of his plans?"

"No sir."

"All right, sergeant. Take care of things here.

The bodies from the fight last night have been returned. We'll have a burial when we get back from the parley."

"Yes, sir." Sgt. Bennedict saluted smartly as the captain dismissed him, then swung his horse around and moved up to the head of the column with the scout, the colonel and the Indian half breed.

Bennedict watched them go. He had already made most of his preparations. Both horses were saddled, another ready with all the provisions he could load on her, including lots of ammunition. He had two rifles and two pistols.

He went to the company orderly's tent and waited. Edgerly should be coming soon. He said he'd be there a half hour after the main party left. Bennedict talked to the orderly about the guard roster and the outlying pickets for the camp defense. They heard pounding hooves and looked up just as Edgerly came to a stop in front of them.

"Sergeant! A band of six Utes working toward camp from the north. I don't know what they're up to."

"You sure they're Indians, Edgerly?"

"Damned right! I know an injun when I see one."

"Edgerly, I don't think it's anything to worry about. Go tell Sgt. Wilson to get me two more men and you can show us where you saw them. Most likely just a hunting party."

Five minutes later, Edgerly and Sgt. Bennedict rode away from the camp, their pack horse in tow. Nobody thought anything about it. The word was they were checking out a hunting party to the north. Both men chuckled as they rode over a small rise in the valley and wound along a small tributary to the larger river. They were soon out of sight in a row of low hills where they picked up their speed.

"Three rivers north, the map showed," Edgerly said.

"I know that, I can read," Bennedict snapped. "Remember, I'm putting twenty years of service on the line here. If we don't find the damn mine, we're coming back and laying out the best damn lie you ever did hear about being ambushed by some renegades. You got that straight, Edgerly?"

"Yeah, I got it straight. And until then we've got no sergeant and no private here. We're by-god partners, and I don't want you giving me any fucking orders!"

Sgt. Bennedict nodded. "Right you are, partners in a gold mine! How does that sound to you? Now let's get our asses in motion, so we can find the place and get to working it. Those Utes are going to be off their feed for a few days while this parley takes place, and things get back to normal. Should be plenty of time for us to get the rest of the gold and strike out for Denver."

"Yeah, lots of gold, let's make tracks!"

Spur led the main party slowly up the gentle valley. He wanted to be sure the Utes knew they were coming, and that they were coming in peace. A private led the way with a large white flag. Actually it was half a bedsheet off Lt. Windsgong's bunk. The sheet had been tied securely to a six foot long guideon and held in place by the fitting on the saddle.

Directly behind the flag rode Spur and Istas. She wore her Indian dress over her shirt and pants, and rode with ease and confidence.

"Nervous?" Spur asked her.

Istas shook her head. "No. These are my people. I lived with them for a year. The old woman who tried to stop us from getting Bessie had befriended me when I was with the tribe when I was twelve. She let me sleep in her tepee in the cold weather. I told her to scream fiercely when I left after we rescued Bessie or they would punish her."

"She certainly did that." They rode in silence for a while. "What do you think Spotted Tail will do?"

"He has little choice. He will be looking at sixty or seventy guns. We know he has only twenty-five, maybe thirty braves, and not all of those have rifles. He must be extremely short on ammunition. Spotted Tail is one of the more intelligent of the Indian chiefs. He'll see the wisdom of compromising."

"So he can save face, how many horses should I offer?"

"Start with one horse for each girl, then work up to three. Any more than three and he would take them but he would have no respect for you."

"Why is that?"

"Old Indian saying that no squaw is worth more than three horses." She laughed.

Spur looked over at her. "There is no way I would sell you for three horses," Spur said.

She looked at him quickly, then realized he was joking, and they laughed again. "Spur McCoy. If you owned me, I would be so good to you, so delicious and irreplaceable, that you would not be able to give me up, let alone want to sell me."

"I can't give you up now," he said, his words more serious than he intended. They both looked away.

Spur did not anticipate a long march. The chief would want the parley to take place as far from his camp as practical. Spur guessed they were only a mile past the ambush point when three Indian appeared from the brush to their left, rode into the grassy valley and stopped two hundred yards from the troops.

Spur gave the orders and the cavalry executed one of its most showy and practical maneuvers, a company front. In this movement the two's or four's swing alternately to the right and left and form a single long line of soldiers facing the enemy.

McCoy signalled the troops to hold fast while he and Istas and the white flag bearer rode out to meet the three Indians. When they came within twenty feet of each other both stopped.

Spur spoke at once.

"Oh great Chief Spotted Tail of the Ute nation," Spur said.

Istas in a strong voice translated it.

"We wish to speak with you about a serious problem." Again the translation came. The first party had spoken.

Spotted Tail stared at them for a moment, then he motioned forward with his hand, and both groups walked toward each other until the noses of their horses were only a foot apart.

The chief looked at the girl closely.

"Istas," he said.

She chattered something in reply, then he sobered. He spoke for a moment and paused, letting Istas translate.

"The Ute nation have no idea why the Great White Chief has sent a thousand guns to stare their deadly eyes at the peaceful Utes."

Spur smiled. "There are two white girls in the winter camp of Spotted Tail. Their families want them back."

After the translations Spotted Tail seemed surprised. "Any white squaws in my camp are the rightful and legal property of the braves who won them in sacred battle."

"That is the law according to the Ute nation," Spur said. "The Great Chief Spotted Tail knows that the Utes must live by their own laws, but they must also live by the laws of the round-eyes. Every year there are more and more roundeyes. Chief Spotted Tail is wise in his belief that the Utes must learn to live side by side with the roundeyes."

The translation continued.

Chief Spotted Tail looked into the woods and then down the river. "I see no round eyes being

179

bothered by the Ute nation. Why do you come and bother my people with such small and unimportant matters?"

"Chief, to the mothers of the white girls, the safety of their daughters, the lives of their loved ones, are tremendously important. I have received instructions all the way from the Great White Father in Washington to come and talk to you about this serious violation of the roundeye law."

"Squaws are this important to the round eyes?"

"The white men hold their women in high esteem. We pamper them and spoil them. It is simply our way."

"Squaws are not important to the Indian. The Ute brave may have three or four squaws, if he can support them because he is a good hunter and warrior."

"Then if squaws are not important, white squaws must be even less valuable."

"This is true."

"Chief Spotted Tail. I too am a chief. I command these hundred round eye Blue Coats. As one chief to another, how can we solve this problem that has bothered both our camps?"

"The braves who own the white squaws would never give them away to the round eyes."

Spur had been waiting for such an opening. He could barely keep from replying until Istas finished translating. But he hesitated. He looked away and shrugged. "Since the white squaws are not important, and since we both have our people to consider, I will offer to buy the squaws from their owners. I will give one sturdy, well trained army horse for each white squaw."

McCoy watched the Indian closely as the translation was made. There was not the flicker of emotion on the granite chiseled features of Spotted Tail.

He looked at Spur and shook his head. "It is a sad day when chiefs have to parley about such an unimportant matter as two white squaws. But, to help keep the peace and prevent any more bloodshed on either side, my braves will give up the white squaws for five army mounts each."

For ten minutes they haggled. At last the bargain was struck: three army horses and three army blankets for each girl.

The chief turned to the brush from which he had ridden and gave a signal. At once the two white girls walked into the open. Spur had an impulse to bolt toward them on his horse and pick them up. But he sat still. The girls walked and then ran forward.

"Hello, I'm Priscilla Patterson," the older girl said. "I understand you've been looking for me."

"Good morning, Miss Patterson. I'm Colonel McCoy. Your uncle sends his good wishes. Just stand fast. We will have you free in a few moments."

He gave a signal and Captain Landower rode up with the string of six horses.

Chief Spotted Tail looked at McCoy sharply for a moment, then he smiled. Spur asked the

Captain to go back and bring six army blankets from the troopers.

When the blankets were spread on the six horses, Chief Spotted Tail nodded and the two Indians beside him whooped, gathered up the rope bridals of the six mounts and rode up the valley with them.

The chief looked at Spur.

"Ute nation want to live in peace with the white man." He spoke in English and Spur was surprised.

"Chief, most white men want to live in peace as well. But there are some bad ones among us who will make that hard." He was about to leave when he hesitated and frowned.

"Chief, your English is very good. It is my wish I could speak the Ute tongue so well."

Spotted Tail nodded, unused to compliments from whites.

"One last request," Spur said on an impulse. "We know about the placer mine to the north." He paused for Istas to translate. "We request the right to work the diggings for one week. At the end of that time, we will take down the sluice way, destroy the evidence of a mine, and return the creek to its natural state. I ask this to aid one of the girls who was rejected first by your people when she was two years old, and, as I'm sure was your custom, left in a snowbank to die."

The chief looked at Istas when the translation was finished.

"Istas," he said and paused. "You have grown into a remarkable woman. Tell the round eye colonel permission is granted, and that the Ute nation made a mistake when they let you get away from us when you came back at your twelfth summer."

She translated, and tears were in her eyes as she looked up at the great chief.

"Thank you, Chief Spotted Tail," she said in his language. The Chief nodded, turned and rode away toward the brush. Spur dismounted, and walked back to the main troop with the two girls. Both wore simple squaw dresses. One was sun-brown from the outdoors life, but the other one was still starkly white. Istas got down from her mount and walked beside them.

She knew exactly what to say to them, but somehow she couldn't find the words. Those were her people who had captured them.

As soon as they turned toward the troop, a horseman raced from the group and charged up to the girls. The man leaped off the horse and ran up to the younger girl. The scout fell to his knees and held out his arms.

The girl cried out and rushed into his arms. Spur stopped and waited. Tears of joy streamed down Lawson Kirk's face as he hugged the daughter he feared he would never see again. They sat for several minutes, holding each other and alternately crying and laughing, then stood and walked hand in hand back to the line of soldiers.

Scouts who had been working both sides of the valley, rode in with a body draped over a horse. Spur rode to meet them.

"It's Lt. Windsong," the private said. "Hasn't

been dead more than an hour or two."

Spur told them to report to Captain Landower, then he rode back to find Istas and Priscilla chattering away like old friends. The three white girls were lodged in the lieutenant's tent along with Istas. It was decided that the troop would stay the night there and in the morning they would strike out for the nearest point of the railroad that had a station.

The captain studied his map and decided that would be Ogden. They would travel cross country to Logan and go down the road south to Ogden, about three days travel away.

That night there was more than they could eat. Hunters had brought down two fat buck deer and they had been cooling out for four hours. The men sang around the fires, and the girls and the scout and the two officers talked and sipped coffee in the big tent talking quietly.

Istas cornered Spur early in the evening.

"What's this about the placer gold mine?"

"The old miner told me to put it to good use. We will. You are going to have to help me. We will work the placer for a week, and do what we promised Chief Spotted Tail. He will keep his braves away from us. You're going to need a stake when you land in St. Louis. You need clothes and a place to stay, and you said you wanted to get more schooling . . ."

She stood close to him. There was surprise, and disbelief and so much love and joy in her face that she could hardly contain it.

"If there weren't so many people around I would kiss you!"

"Later," he said. "We'll have a whole week. And you may not get all of the money. If there is any chance that Bessie can't get back into her family, we'll leave a dowry for her with the sheriff. So we have a lot to work for."

Istas touched his shoulder. "You are a wonderfully beautiful human being. Do you know that, McCoy?" she grinned and walked over to talk to the Mormon girl, Bessie.

They would be up at five A.M., so the small party broke up early in the officer's tent. Everyone said goodnight and Captain Landower posted two guards at the girls' tent.

Spur had been sleeping for some time when he sensed someone moving in the dark tent. He tensed, reaching for his pistol. A small soft hand closed around his wrist.

"Easy," a woman's voice whispered. "I didn't sneak in here just to be shot."

Spur recognized Priscilla's voice.

"Outside," she said softly. "We need to talk."

Spur lifted from his blankets and they slipped out of the tent without waking Captain Landower.

Outside she caught his hand, faded into a shadow and moved without a sound. Soon they were in the moonlight shadows of the tall pine trees.

She turned around and smiled.

"Now, what do we have to talk about that was so urgent?" Spur asked the remarkably attractive young woman.

CHAPTER SIXTEEN

THE SENATOR'S DAUGHTER smiled at Spur McCoy in the moonlight under the tall pine trees.

"You don't remember me and I'm crushed. We met in Washington several years ago. You haven't changed, but I have, thank God. I was a flat chested string bean of thirteen."

"I would have remembered you," Spur said.

"Nope. You were trying to court my older sister that evening. I don't think you got her to bed. She said you didn't."

Priscilla moved close to him, leaned her body against his and reached up and kissed his lips. She came back and kissed him again, then put her arms around him and pushed her hips hard against his.

She ended the kiss and stared at him. "Now, Spur McCoy, I want to be sure you remember me this time."

She took his hand and pushed it down the unbuttoned front of the army shirt. She wore nothing under it.

"There's no need for you to do this," he said softly.

"Maybe I have some needs too," she said.

186

His hand closed on a breast and she sighed.

"Now I feel like I have been rescued. A good man petting my boobies is the greatest feeling in the world. Let's sit down in the grass."

They sat down and she put his hand back where it was. Her hand moved to his crotch and then his fly and slowly unbuttoned it.

"I bet you think I'm just awful making the advances."

"No, I'm enjoying it, but as I said, you don't have to."

"I want to, goddamnit! Can't you understand that some women like sex just as much as men do? I would rather get fucked than do anything else in the world!"

Spur laughed and when he did she wormed her hands inside his pants and found the stiffness there.

"Oh, my! I bet he is a dandy! But he's all bent and crooked. Help me straighten him out!"

Spur undid his belt and the top button and she pulled his pants down until she could get his phallus out of the short underwear so he pointed upward stiff and proud.

"Oh, my yes!" she said, moaning in joy. "He's a pretty prick. May I kiss him hello?"

"Only if I can kiss your beautiful tits first."

She laughed and shrugged out of the army shirt. Her breasts came out boldly, her shoulders back stretching them forward for the best show. Creamy shite skin surged in twin mounds tipped by large aerolas and surging dark pink nipples. His hands petted them, massaged them round and round and she sighed and bent forward a little now so they firmed and surged forward.

Spur bent and kissed around each mound, then licked the hardened nipple and felt them surge taller. He kissed them and then leaned back.

She went down and kissed his turgid penis, cooing to it and humming a small tune, then she kissed the pulsating tip and he almost exploded. But he held control as she slid him into her mouth and sucked for a minute, then she came away and kissed his lips and pushed him on his back.

"I want you all bare! I want to see your fantastic, lean, strong body before you fuck me."

She helped him out of his shirt. He had been sleeping with his boots off, feeling fairly safe in the middle of the army camp. She pulled his pants and short underwear down and sat there staring at him.

"I always like to watch first. Men are so different! I mean so strong, so agile. Muscles. I love them!"

"Did you make love with the Indians?"

"Of course. It was either that or die, and I didn't want to die and I was curious. But there is no difference. An Indian man is just like any other man. A little rougher, but physically . . . She looked at him. "You're fucking Istas, aren't you? I can tell by the way she looks at you. Once a man has shoved his prick inside a girl it . . . it does something to her and it changes the relationship forever. She might not want to admit

188

it, but there is some strange change in even the most casual relationships between two people after fucking."

She took his hand and moved them under her skirt.

"Want to go exploring?"

He rolled over on top of her, kissed her three times, pushed his tongue into her mouth and she whimpered in wonder and joy. His hand worked up her leg and brushed across her bare crotch and then down the other side.

"Don't tease me!" she shouted.

He put his hand over her mouth.

"Easy! You don't want to bring a roving guard out here, do you?"

Her eyes flared and she shook her head. He took his hand away from her mouth.

"Don't worry, we'll get there, at least three times. Why were you in such a hurry? Why get me out here tonight?"

"I thought you might not go on the march back to Ogden with us."

"You're right. We'll be moving the other way, Istas and I."

"I knew you were fucking her. Is she good?"

"Almost as good as you are, and that is fantastic!"

She pushed his hand back to her crotch. "Play with me."

Spur's hand rubbed across her crotch softly and she moaned, pinned his hand there and sighed. "I think you've found the spot."

His finger searched, found her erect clit and he rubbed it back and forth.

"What's that? What is that marvelous, delicious feeling?"

Spur lifted his brows. "You don't know about your clit? This little node down here?"

"Nobody ever told me."

"Let me show you." He rubbed it back and forth a dozen times and suddenly she erupted, wailing, moaning, making little kitten cries as her body shook and rattled and tried to shatter itself.

When the series of spasms had churned through her, she looked up in total disbelief.

"What was that?"

"You just climaxed. Haven't you done that before?"

"No, oh no. But I want to again!" She pushed his hand back in place and tensed as he rubbed her again. She was anticipating it this time and it took only half as many massages on her clit before she rattled into another smashing climax.

Priscilla held her eyes tightly closed as she lay there gasping for breath. She reached out and found his erection and held it with one hand as her breath still came in huge gasps, and a shudder trembled through her now and then. At last her eyelids fluttered and she looked up at him.

Tears of ecstasy sparkled her eyes. She shook her head slowly.

"No one has ever . . . I mean I've never had anyone do . . ." She laughed. "I just fucked them and thought that was it. My God! You mean I've been missing this all those times!"

She sat up her hands on her hips, fire lashed out of her eyes.

"Those goddamn men! Those shit-sucking bastards! All that time they got their jollies, they *cum* as they said, and they never told me I could do this? Jesus, what a batch of bastards you men really are!"

"Hey, easy. I'm the one who showed you . . ."

She swarmed over him, kissing his lips, dropping down and kissing his still hard tool. She chewed on it a minute and then got up on her hands and knees. She looked at him where he sat beside her.

"Darling, baby Spur. Do me a favor?"

"Sure."

"Do me in my little arsehole. Fuck me dirty! I've only let two men do it to me, but I want you to. Some guys get wigged out coming in an asshole. You want mine?"

Spur went on his knees behind her rubbing her soft little bottom. "First time, or second time, or third time in your tight little bung?"

"All three you want, honey-babe. Just git to fucking!"

Spur was surprised how quickly he climaxed. She was giving him all the help she could and a moment later they lay side by side in the grass.

"That was just great!" she said, kissing his arm.

"It gets better. Where are you going when you get to the railroad station?"

"I was heading for San Francisco before. I've never been there, and with the train it's only about a week's ride. Only I found a detour."

"So you'll go back to Washington, D.C."

"I don't see why I should. I'll write a letter telling my parents I was adopted by Chief Spotted Tail as his daughter and he was saving me to sell as a bride for twenty horses, but none of the braves in his tribe could afford me. I'll make it sound like none of the Indians even got a look at one tit."

"Will your parents believe you?"

"My mother will. She's the important one. Daddy won't. He knows about my . . . my enjoyment of men. He caught me with a neighbor boy when we were both fourteen. I had bigger boobs than any of the other girls my age and this boy had a constant hardon. One day my folks were gone and the boy with the big cock slipped over the fence and we played some doctor and nurse. He got my blouse off and was playing with my tits when my father caught us.

"Daddy whipped the boy and sent him running. I had been so fascinated I hadn't covered up. He stared at my tits and the next thing I knew my Daddy was on his knees in front of me kissing my big boobs and jacking off right there in the back yard. He just got carried away. But he made me promise never to tell mother or anyone. I said I wouldn't tell, if he was a little less strict with me."

"You had the old man over a log!"

"I got lots more pretty clothes, and a watch on a chain, and presents, and the folks were gone lots of Saturdays. The third time they left I had a boy over and we both undressed and really examined each other. He ejaculated as soon as I took off my clothes. I'd never seen it happen before. We fooled around but not much else happened."

"But the next time?"

"The next time I got fucked out of my virginity. It didn't hurt at all, and I kind of liked it. I got all warm and hot and feeling good." She grinned and kissed him. "But, Jesus! Nothing like this!" She kissed him again and rolled on top of him. "Do it again to me, again and again. Only this time I want to be on top!"

It was almost dawn when Spur helped Priscilla slip into her tent and he stretched out on his blankets on the floor of the captain's digs. He would sleep only until the bugle called, then be ready to go. It had been one hell of an exhausting night.

Six miles to the north, across three good sized ridges, two ex-cavalrymen worked at the sluice trough. They had got a half a day in yesterday, and were hard at it this morning.

"Damnit, Bennedict, I need more water through here. The big rocks won't wash down, and that means we need more water."

"Pick out the damn things by hand and throw them away," Bennedict said. "I got all the flow we can get without digging a bigger pond. You want to do that?"

"Okay, don't get talking like a damn sergeant again. We'll just have to let it wash longer. Come look at this dust we got."

They had taken out the dust in front of the baffles that had washed out since the old miner was taken away by the Indians. They put it in a tin pot so it would dry out. They both stared at the pot and as well as into a second one they had put the new gold dust in, dust that they had scraped from the baffles that morning. It was still wet. They spread it around to dry. Then it would go into leather pouches they had brought with them.

Bennedict slapped his leg and whistled.

"Damn! We must be getting close to three pounds of dust! That is almost a thousand damn dollars. We'd both sweat in the army for four years to make five hundred each!"

Former Private Olson ran his fingers through the dust and shook his head.

"Almost too much to believe. How much longer can we work before McCoy and the Utes come and check?"

"Another three days, I figure. Today they probably give up the girls to that colonel. Or maybe yesterday. They will be getting back to their normal hunting routine."

"Hell, we better do it then. Tonight we'll pile in more sand than usual so the all night water can wash it down."

Olson went with him and they shoveled up a little dam across part of the three foot wide stream to divert more water toward their sluice opening. It was hard work.

By noon they had worked the first two batches through the sluice. They didn't let the wet gold dust dry a bit, just scraped it free with the inch-wide putty knife they had found there, and Olson took over the digging into the trench alongside the stream where the gold bearing sand lay in a thick strata.

"Must have been collecting there for a thousand years," Bennedict said. "Look at that, you can even see it glimmer in the sunlight!"

Olson dropped the shovel and fell to his knees. He picked up something from the bottom of the trench and polished it. Then he held it up and screeched.

"Jeeeeeeeeeesus! Look at this! A nugget! A gold nugget!"

Bennedict ran over to him and looked at it. It was a nugget, about the size of a marble, not round but polished and smooth on one side and rough on the other.

Bennedict held out his hand and Olson gave it to him.

"Mighty nice, Olson. Remember, we share everything. You want it, you can buy out my half."

"Fuck you, Bennedict! I found it. This one is mine. You want one, you find one." They both scrambled back into the trench and pawed at the ground, but could find no more nuggets. After a while they both laughed and sat down in the trench.

"Now I know what they mean by gold fever," Bennedict said. "It hits a man like the strike of a rattler, and there is no cure."

He gave the nugget back to Olson who grinned and pocketed it.

"I better go up and tend to my water," Bennedict said. Olson heaved a sigh, and went back to shoveling gold bearing sand and gravel into the twenty foot length of the flume that was six inches deep with water.

A half hour later he was finished with the careful placement of the sand. He sat and watched the water doing its work, going into the flume clear and pure enough to drink, but coming out the far end, as dirty and dank as a muddy bucket.

Bennedict leaned on his shovel. There was no chance he was going to share the gold with an idiot like Olson. He had picked the big, sturdy private carefully. He had a strong back, and not much of a mind to go with it. The sooner they got the placer work done, the sooner Olson would find out for sure if there was any life after death.

Bennedict knew there wasn't. He was going to get his right here and enjoy it, and let the preachers scream and rant and rave all they wanted to.

He grinned thinking how he had lied to Olson about how long they could work the placer. He had figured two days, including yesterday. The Utes would have more scouts out than usual, and they certainly would cover this valley every other day.

So tonight Olson would meet his maker, so to speak, and Hirum Bennedict, lately of the U.S. Army and now a man of means, would move out toward the trail that led to Denver. Denver! It was a rough town but with plenty of luxuries. He was going to buy two, no three of those female luxuries for his first night in town!

He was thinking so hard about what he would

do with all the money, that he never saw Olson move up behind him.

Olson was strong, and he swung the shovel like a club, aiming for the sergeant's rib cage as the biggest target. The shovel slammed into Bennedict just as he turned, otherwise it would have broken six ribs and driven them through his heart.

Bennedict screamed and clawed for his six-gun. They had agreed not to use their firearms for any reason, since the sound might alert the Ute nearby. He felt the terrible pain in his side, and knew that he had two or three broken ribs. He tumbled to the ground and tore at his holster. The cumbersome U.S. Army holster was difficult to get into. The pain was roaring in his ears. He saw Olson raise the shovel again.

Bennedict drew the .45 pistol and fired one shot. It caught the private in the chest, too high for his heart, but through the top of his lung. The force of the round staggered Olson back. He caught at his own pistol and fired wildly, then stumbled as he moved cautiously downstream toward the sluice and the trench of gold.

"Thought you'd take all the gold, did you, Olson!" Bennedict cried out. He leveled his pistol but a wave of nausea swept over him and he turned and vomited. His chest and insides must be hurt more than he thought.

He aimed again, but by then Olson was in the trench which gave him total protection. He was in an ideal defensive position.

Bennedict wiped his mouth and then his eyes. He reached over and took several mouthfuls of water from the stream, and tried to figure out what to do.

Ordinarily a simple tactical problem such as this would be solved in seconds, and he would send the right men to do the job. Now he was the only man. He wished he had a hand bomb, or even some half sticks of dynamite. He threw a rock at the trench, groaning as the movement caused great distress along his rib cage.

"Olson, you traitor! You're hit bad, dying. Don't you want me to at least come down there and sit with you?"

There was no response. Bennedict took that to mean his traitorous partner was in worse condition than he had thought. He held the pistol in one hand, his shovel in the other as a crutch, stood and moved slowly forward.

He had about fifteen yards to negotiate. With each step he watched the edge of the trench where Olson had vanished.

Nothing.

He took another step and his side filled with pain that made his gasp and close his eyes to fight it down. When he opened his eyes he looked at the trench and saw Olson standing, both hands holding a .45 revolver that pointed directly at Bennedict.

The muzzle belched smoke and flame and a small dark object seemed to rocket toward Bennedict. He knew he should move, but no messages were getting to his legs. The black object came nearer and nearer and then smashed into the ex-sergeant's right cheek, drove upward through the roof of his mouth and broke into five fragments, each tearing into vital life-response centers of his brain.

Ex-Sergeant Hirum Bennedict fell backward over a pile of shale, his arms extending outward in shock and then locked there in death as he sprawled on his back, his head touching the swiftly running little stream.

Private Olson watched his former sergeant die, and he wanted to laugh, but he could barely breathe. He had been spitting up blood. Each attempt to pull air into his lungs caused him the most terrible pain he had ever imagined. He sat down on the edge of the trench and leaned on the trough.

The blackness that came lasted only a moment, then was gone. He reached into the swiftly flowing water in the sluice and splashed water on his face.

Yes! it felt so good. He let the pistol drop. There was no need for it now. He splashed more water on his face. Then to his surprise he had trouble lifting his hands. His right hand totally failed to respond next. It wouldn't move. He tried his left hand and it also had frozen in place.

A rainbow of lights danced around his head, and when he tried to turn away from them, he couldn't.

For a moment he was terrified. Then it all seemed so right. He had killed the bastard Sgt. Bennedict who had talked in his sleep last night about his plans to do away with Olson. It was a matter of doing Bennedict in first. He should have used his pistol after all, made sure.

The blackness came again and with it a

sudden rushing. Strange, he thought. Then Olson looked down and saw the water in the sluice only an inch from his face, and his whole head was moving downward.

The water touched his nose, and he tried to take a breath. Then the water rose up to his eyes, and he closed them and with a soft sigh of relief let his head sink six inches into the water which kept flowing over the baffles. He looked through the water and the last things Pvt. Olson saw were a million glints as the sun bounced off the gold on the baffle three inches from his eyes. Time had ended for Pvt. Olson.

CHAPTER SEVENTEEN

SPUR MCCOY WAS up with the troops that morning and watched the always interesting but somewhat frantic preparations for an army, even a small unit like this, to get on the march after a few days at a camp.

He watched the men and animals scurrying around preparing to leave. It was time for a last talk with Captain Landower.

"Discovered a pair of deserters to go along with your missing jar of gold, Colonel McCoy. Sergeant Bennedict, a twenty year veteran, evidently took private Olson and went after that placer mine the old man worked."

"I may run up against them somewhere today, Captain. If I do I'll certainly give them your compliments."

"On the end of a forty five round I hope. Only way we can figure it is that Bennedict got Lt. Windsong to steal the gold jar out of my tent in exchange for Bennedict cutting the officer loose. It all fits."

The burial detail had been at work and now the bugle sounded the last call for the men.

"I've figured out what to do about

201

Windsong," the Captain said. "I wrote a final report on him last night giving him full credit for rescuing the Patterson girl. I made him a damn hero. Also recommended that he be promoted one grade and given a medal for valor. That should take care of the general."

"But your men know what really happened."

"Why should they talk? Not in this kind of a situation. Nobody will question it. Surely not the top military officers." He shrugged. "What the hell. I've got sixteen years of duty. Four more and I can retire if I want to. I know I'm never going to make general anyway."

Spur took his hand. "I think you've made the right decision. Why let his family know what kind of an ass he really was? This way things will flow smoothly. We got three of the girls out. You did your job in spite of Windsong. And Spotted Tail is settled down. He isn't going to confront the army, at least not for a long time."

Captain Landower saluted Spur. "Thanks, Colonel McCoy. We'll get the girls and the troops on into Ogden where we all get on the train and ride back to Camp Pilot Butte. That's going to be the best part of our patrol. And you're going gold mining. Good luck. I'll send that telegram for you first thing when we hit the station in Ogden."

The troopers were formed up ready to leave. A sergeant came riding up, reported as Spur waved and swung away to where Istas sat on her horse waiting. They both had fat sacks of supplies tied behind their saddles, enough food for two weeks.

Istas smiled as he rode up. She touched his shoulder and pointed to the two girls who waved from the back of the supply wagon. Spur and Istas waved back, then turned and rode north.

"The third valley?" Spur asked.

"Yes, but I hear we may have company up there, the two deserters."

"If they're smart they will take the gold and run as far and as fast as they can."

"And leave the rest of the gold just laying there in the sand? I bet they're still there."

"Then we'll have to take time out for a long talk with them."

"They'll be talking with bullets."

Spur grinned. "I hope they are."

They rode for an hour and a half, over one ridge after another, then looked down into the third valley from the ridgeline.

It was a smaller valley than the others and twisted and turned to the west. They rode along the ridgeline watching below, hoping for a surprise.

For fifteen minutes they worked along the ridgeline, found a game trail and dropped down on the forward slope about twenty yards and found easier riding. Through a patch of heavier timber they came out on light growth and there ahead and to the right they saw the little camp, the scar on the land of the digging and the sluice box.

They also saw two men both in unnatural positions. Neither moved. One lay with his head half in the shallow creek, the other bent over the sluice with his head down as if examining it closely.

"Let's go!" Spur said and they worked down the slope and rode up the last few yards. Neither man had moved since Spur had seen them.

Spur could see the man at the sluice clearly. His face was underwater. The Secret Service agent lifted the face from the water. It was not bloated, dead only a few hours. He moved the body to the ground and went to look at the second man. He was dead too, and still wearing his sergeant stripes, Bennedict.

They found the pots of gold dust now almost dry in the sun.

Spur took a shovel and went to a soft spot nearby and buried the two men in the same grave and filled it in. Four men had died because of this little placer operation. There would be no more if he could help it.

He went back to the trough where Istas sat watching the water tumble over the baffles. He looked closely and saw a build-up of gold on each baffle.

"There must be a shut-off somewhere to stop the water coming through," he said. "Then we dig out the gold dust." He found the small gate across the sluice box and closed it, then noticed the putty knife near one of the pots of gold. Using it and another pan he began cleaning the gold dust from the baffle where the water had stopped rushing past.

"Let me help," Istas said. He gave her the putty knife and her eyes went wide as she began cleaning the wet gold dust off the wooden baffle.

Spur examined the little camp. He found the deserters' horses, three of them, and the heavy pack of supplies. They would have plenty to eat. He collected the rifles and pistols and put them in a stack. The jar of gold with the map still inside lay with the other equipment.

Before he buried the two men he had seen a glint of gold between the private's fingers. When he pried the fingers apart he had found the gold nugget. He put it in his pocket. Now he took it out and looked at it. With a little work a jeweler could fashion it into an interesting pendant. He put the nugget in the jar of gold, and went back to the placer operation. Spur found the pond and the sluice gate which had increased the flow of water through the box.

"I'm done," Istas called. He went back to the box, and checked out the digging area. He could see glints of gold in the sand. At once he picked up the shovel and began scooping sand into the box. He was not sure how much to put in, or how long it would take to wash the dirt and gravel away and catch the gold. The first bunch of sand he put in the sluice box was a trial. It washed out in about an hour so he decided he should use more sand. After three tries he had it about right.

They stopped when the sun was directly overhead and made dinner, coarse bread, marmelade, coffee and some berries that Istas had found.

"Tomorrow we'll have fresh meat," she told him.

They could use their guns to hunt, since Spotted Tail had given them permission to be there. Spur felt sure there would be scouts watching them from time to time, but they would be observing only.

In the afternoon they scraped out the gold dust and dug more sand and gravel, and Spur began to appreciate how hard the placer miners worked for the gold dust.

Istas had the dry dust all cleaned of rocks or sand and stored in foot-long leather pouches she had found in the deserter's equipment. She figured they had about four pounds of dust. Soberly she also realized that four men already died producing it.

When it got dark and they could work the trough no more, they went up the slope and made a small camp. They fell into their blankets without eating, too tired to more than kiss each other and snuggle together before they fell asleep.

In the morning Istas asked Spur what had happened to the two deserters. Spur had inspected the wounds before he buried the men.

"Looks like they had an argument and shot each other. The sergeant had bashed in ribs too, as if he had been hit hard by something. Maybe that started it and then the shooting followed. The private evidently died slower, and fell into the water and either drowned or was dead when he hit the water."

"And no one will ever know. What about their families?"

"Most enlisted men in the army have few strong family ties. For lots of them, the army is their family. I'll put an item in my report about Bennedict and Olson, and the army can clear them off their books as being dead and no longer deserters."

They were working as soon as the sun came up, hugging hot cups of coffee in the chill of the thin air at over 4,500 feet.

At noon, Spur had just filled the trough with a fresh serving of sand and he took Istas's hand and led her to their blankets and sat down.

"A rest time," he said and stretched out on the blankets on his back. She hovered over him and when he opened his eyes, she kissed him.

"I've missed you," she said.

"Two days, maybe three."

"Too long," she said. She rolled on top of him and kissed him again. "Please, right now, before you use up all of your energy."

They made love under the trees, listening to the softly chattering stream. It was slow and gentle and meaningful.

"St. Louis?" she asked suddenly.

"If you want to go there. My office there can help you get situated and help you find a job."

"Yes, I want to go."

"Good." He kissed her once more, then pulled on his pants and laced up his boots. "Time to work again."

It was a pattern they followed for the five

days they were there. They worked in the morning, made love at noon and then worked again until darkness and fell into their blankets.

The bags of gold dust increased. Toward the end of the next to last day, gold bearing sand was harder to find. At the middle of the last day they washed two batches of sand and found only a trace of gold.

Without a word Spur began to shovel in the trench that had been dug along the stream. He had it half-filled with debris from the dig when the water broke in and filled it. He found a hammer in the old men's camp, and pounded the trough and the higher flume into pieces, and stacked the boards out of sight under some trees.

Before darkness, the place looked like almost any other part of the canyon along the small stream.

That night they checked the bags of gold dust in the firelight.

Spur judged them and kept track. "I'd guess we have about twenty pounds of gold dust."

"There can't be that much!"

"Looks like there is. You're a rich young lady, Istas Smith."

She looked up quickly. "I don't want to use that name."

Spur nodded. "Fine, you can use any name you like. You can even change your first name if you want to."

"No, I want to stay Istas, that's part of me. But not Smith. He threw me out. Patterson. I want to be Istas Patterson, like the pretty girl, Priscilla!''

Spur smiled and kissed her cheek. ''You are now Istas Patterson, and we'll set up all of your bank accounts and credits that way. You're a rich young lady, Istas Patterson!''

She kissed him back and then frowned. ''How much . . . how much is all that gold worth?''

''About six thousand, seven hundred dollars.''

''That's more money than I ever thought existed! Do you know that before you came, I would live for weeks and never see more than fifteen or twenty cents!'' She put her arms around him and seemed contented just to be there, close to him.

''What ever would I have done without you!''

He held her, knowing there was nothing to say. They let the fire burn down. In the morning they would ride back toward Ogden, a summing up and a parting. They stretched out and still in each other's arms, went to sleep.

Spur was up with the sun, dismantling the last of the old miners' camp, catching the horses which he had let wander in the small valley. They packed the rifles and equipment the miners had used on one pack horse, then tied the other mounts in a string behind it, and moved out toward Ogden. They cut across country to hit the horse trail that angled due south. A westerly course would cross it.

Three days later they rode into Ogden. Spur took two rooms at the Railway Hotel. He found out that the army patrol had arrived there and shipped out on an eastbound train five days earlier. Spur went to the one local bank that accepted gold dust and wrangled with them for an hour about the purity. At last he accepted a ninety-five percent figure and the bank weighed out the gold. There were twenty-two pounds and twelve ounces.

The gold was worth $7523.88, less the five percent for foreign matter, it came to $7,147.68. Spur put $4,000 in an account at the Smith Bank of Ogden, took a letter of credit made out to Miss Istas Patterson for $2,500 and asked for the rest, $647.68 in cash. When the transactions were completed, the day was nearly over and Spur went back to the hotel.

He found Istas in his bedroom standing before a mirror. At first he didn't recognize her. She wore a shimmering white dress that showed off her figure and swept to her ankles. The long white sleeves were capped by white gloves, and a pert white and gold hat perched on her head.

She turned. "Like it?" she asked.

"It's wonderful!" Spur said. He ran to her and picked her up and swung her around. "And now it's time to go to dinner."

"Oh, no, this is for an evening at the opera. I have another outfit to use for dinner."

They went down the hall to her room and she changed quickly, putting the white dress back in a box almost reverently. Then she put on a blue dress with puff sleeves and that swept the floor in the current fashion, but was less showy. She held out her hand.

"Shall we go to the dining room?" she asked.

They had dinner and he told her about the money, and she nearly shouted in joy and surprise.

Spur had inquired about Bessie. Captain Landower had insisted that he would return the girl only to her parents, and they had a long conference in the captain's hotel room, that ended in a tearful reunion. The family had agreed to take her back in all good faith and promised that they would not let her capture in any way affect how they or the community treated her. Spur made several inquiries and it seemed the family and Ogden were keeping their promises.

As they finished the meal, Spur told her that a train would be coming through at noon the next day.

"I should wait another day," she said. "To get used to this idea that I have some money and that I am a real person."

"Afraid?"

"Terribly! You're the one person who has treated me like a person in all my adult life. How will I know who to trust? What if the lady from your St. Louis office doesn't meet me? What if I lose my money on the train?"

"Istas Patterson. Look at me. You are terrific! You'll never lose your determination and your spunk! Nothing else matters. You are going to be fine in St. Louis. I'll telegraph my office there and somebody will meet you. Tomorrow?"

She sighed and nodded. "I had a bath this

afternoon and washed my hair and . . . just everything. I feel so . . . so different! Do you know this is the first time I've ever been inside this hotel, and the first time that I've ever eaten supper here!"

"It's about time. Now I have two important things to do. First I need to send a telegram before the office closes, and then I want to have a long heart to heart talk with Ezekiel Smith."

"Can I come along?"

Spur grinned. "You deserve to be there, but we wouldn't say a word if you were along. I need to make an impression on his mind, one way or the other."

They went back up to her room and she unlocked the door. "You may give me a small kiss on the cheek if you wish." She giggled. "See how prim and proper I am becoming."

"Good, we'll have a talk about that, too." He kissed her cheek, then her nose. "Now get inside. I'll come see you when I get back."

"If you see Ruth, say hello to her for me. And thank her for all of those dinners. Sometimes that was all that kept me alive, just waiting for that note telling me to come see her."

"I'll tell her, if I can without Mr. Smith hearing. Now off you go."

CHAPTER EIGHTEEN

SPUR STOPPED AT the telegraph office and pounded on the door until the operator opened it up.

"Special United States business," Spur told him. He wrote out the message and gave it to the key man. He addressed it to go to Washington D.C. to Capital Investigations. It said:

"Ute kidnapping party over. Have tied up all loose ends. Contacting St. Louis office for next priority. Give Senator Patterson my regards."

The second wire went to St. Louis. It said:

"Fleurette Leon, meet Istas Patterson on train arriving there from Utah in two days. Find her local lodging. Put her to work in office until a suitable job can be found for her. Take care of her. She is your sister! You are responsible. Wire at once care of Ogden Railroad Hotel the next three highest priority missions."

After he had sent both wires, Spur paid the old telegrapher, who looked up through his wirerimmed glasses.

"You the gent who struck it rich in the gold mines?"

"I work with the government, sir!" Spur said

with all the disdain that he could muster. "I certainly am not a prospector!" He turned and marched out of the office.

He grinned as soon as he was outside. The gold story would be around, but these Mormons would not flash into gold fever and rush into the hills. He would plant the stories about the four men who died at the placer mine, which was worked out. Also he would let it out that the Utes promised to boil the brains of any miner caught on their hunting grounds.

He walked down several blocks to the Ezekiel Smith house and knocked on the door.

Ezekiel answered and when he saw who it was his face froze.

"What are you doing here?" the Mormon leader asked.

"I need to talk with you, Mr. Smith. Inside or out here in the street, I don't care which one."

Reluctantly Smith opened the door and let him in. Smith stood in the hallway, not offering him a chair. He crossed his arms across his chest and waited.

"I thought you might be interested to know that your former daughter, Istas, was primarily responsible for freeing the three white girls from the Ute Indians."

Smith took a long breath. "It is good that they are free."

"I also have heard that you advised Bessie's family not to accept her back from the army now that she has been freed from her captivity by the Ute Indians. Just how do you defend that, Mr. Smith?"

"I don't have to defend it."

"You might not have to defend the actions to yourself, or your fellow Mormons, but you sure as hell have to tell me why. And you are going to tell me right now." Spur still wore the .45 on his belt and one hand fell to his side near the holster.

Smith looked down at the gun, then back at the stern, almost angry expression on his federal man's face.

"It is none of your affair. It is the jurisdiction and the responsibility of the church. It is a moral affair, and you have no business interfering."

"Oh, but I do, Mr. Smith. I have seen fifteen United States cavalrymen die in the effort to rescue those girls. I know that two civilians also died in the process as well as some Indians. I am placing that blood on your head, Smith. And you damn well better give me some explanations. The family accepted the girl back as a daughter, with full and total love and affection. Do you think that you are a superior being to the Indian?"

Smith scowled, started to say something, then stopped. "Yes," he answered.

"Why? Can you run faster, jump farther? Can you shoot straighter? Are you any more honorable or just than they are? Haven't you cast out a daughter as *unfit* the same way they do? How are you better?"

"I am a Mormon, a saint, a son of God."

"Well, hot damn! Ain't you something? If Mormons turn thirteen year old girls into the streets, deny them food and clothing and even the simplest of existence, for any damn reason, I'd say I don't want anything ever to do with a Mormon again."

"That's unfair."

"So are you unfair, sir! If this is your religion, I want no part of it. And right now I am telling you I think you should be forced to live the way Istas did for nine years, grubbing for a meal, no warm clothes, no bed, no love or affection. You should be put in a damn cage for nine years and live on scraps from the plates of the dogs!"

"Get out of my house!"

Spur saw movement behind the Mormon. Skirts fluttered and were gone.

"I'll leave this contaminated pig sty when I'm ready. Now I want to give you a warning. I have eyes and ears in Ogden. If ever I hear that Bessie has been pushed around, slighted in any way, discriminated against, I will come back here and tear your lying tongue out of your mouth and then slowly strangle you until your eyes bulge out and your voice cracks a last apology. This is not a polite warning. This is a threat! Do you understand me, you ridiculous excuse for a man?"

Smith's hands were fisting at his sides. His breath came in short, angry gasps. He started to lift his hands.

"Go ahead, take one swing at me you, bastard, and I'll have the excuse to beat you into a bloody, stinking pulp!"

Smith dropped his hands at once, slid around

Spur and opened the door. He would not look at Spur.

"Smith, if I were you, I'd make it my special duty to see that Bessie has a marvelous catch as a first wife, that she gets special treatment by the church and its members because of her ordeal. I'd do that if I were you, Smith. Because that's one way you can guarantee that you will not suffer a tragic and early death with the most terrible pain imaginable. Because that's what I will do to you if I hear of Bessie having any problems."

Spur turned and moved out of the house, down the walk and to the street. He saw window curtains flutter in the Smith house as he moved away into the darkness.

At the first alley he saw a woman hurrying toward the street. She waved at him and he stopped. When she came up to him in the dim light, he saw that she was Ruth Smith, Ezekiel's third wife.

"Mr. McCoy, could I have a word with you?" She motioned him down the alley. When they came to a spot that was dark, she stopped and smiled at him.

"I just want to shake your hand. I've never heard anyone upbraid Ezekiel that way, and the world knows that he has deserved it from time to time. How is Istas? Is she well? Where is she? What is she going to do?"

Spur smiled. This was a most attractive lady. He touched her shoulder. "Easy. Istas is fine. She has a room at the Railroad Hotel under her new name Istas Patterson. You can go there tonight or tomorrow morning and see her."

Quickly he told her about Istas, how she followed him, and took him to the winter camp, and everything that happened since.

Ruth smiled. "She is such a marvelous little lady, in spite of everything that has happened to her. I am thrilled about the money. After doing without so much for so long, she is a most deserving person."

"She said you kept her alive time after time. She loves you like a mother."

"Even though she is a year older than I am." Ruth paused. "I shouldn't be blabbering this way. I wanted to thank you for what you did for Bessie. I know her. I'm so glad she survived." She paused, then hurried on as if she had made up her mind. "Do you have a few moments? There is something I'd like to show you."

"Yes, this was my last stop for the day."

She smiled, and led him along the alley until she was behind the Ezekiel Smith home. There was a small stable and a stable house over it. She flashed him a smile and went to the narrow stairs that went up to the rooms overhead.

"Up here," she said softly. "I'd appreciate it if you could be quiet."

They went up the dark steps, and into a small room without windows. There was a narrow bed, a chair and a book of Mormon on a stand.

"This is a chamber where we come when we are upset and need to be by ourselves. Ezekiel also uses it as a place to send a child who has misbehaved and needs punishment. There is a lock on the inside, but none outside. She fumbled for a moment, then struck a match and lighted a small lamp. Ruth went to the door and threw the bolt.

"You wanted to show me something?"

She smiled. "Yes. In a way. I want to thank you for helping Istas, and I could think of only one thing I have I could give you that would show you the depth of my appreciation." She turned toward the lamp for a moment and when she swung around, the front of her dress was open. She held the dress apart so he could see her breasts that were high and full with heavy nipples.

"Mr. McCoy, I want to give myself to you." She caught one of his hands and put it on her warm breasts. She gasped when his flesh touched hers, then smiled and drew him toward the bed.

She sat on the bed and pushed the dress off her shoulders, then unbuttoned the fasteners down to the bottom.

Spur looked at her in surprise and admiration.

"Are you sure?"

"Oh, yes! And I just hope that you made love to Istas gently and tenderly. She deserves so much." As she talked she took off the rest of her clothes until she sat there naked and waiting.

He started to open his shirt but she touched his hands.

"No, don't undress. This is for you. Do what

you want. Have me do what you want. Anything. Our community owes you and I am going to make good on our debt."

He bent and kissed her breasts and she gasped. Then he kissed them again and chewed on her nipples until he thought they would burst. Her hands opened his fly and urged his erection out.

"Quickly," she said. "I can't be missing for long. He will be furious with everyone the rest of the week."

Spur watched her lie down and then moved over her. He was sure his rough clothing would chafe her, but she smiled and lifted her knees and helped. When he lanced inside her she moaned with a deep growl and climaxed almost at once. She came again and again, and then he found his own resistance was low and they both climaxed together and then lay there in each other's arms, panting and breathing hard to get back their breath.

"Much too fast," she said, holding him to her with her arms around his back. "I wish we had more time. But I have satisfied myself by defying the man who insisted on my being his wife. I have defied him this way for the first and last time, but it is so satisfying to me that it will last the rest of my life."

Spur tried to roll away but she held him.

"Do you understand? In this community a third wife is not the favored position. In some households there is a third wife because the first refuses to let her husband sleep with her anymore. Sometimes there are physical problems. Sometimes there is simply a need for more children and more help with those already born. A third wife is low on the totem pole. That's why I glory in defying him whenever I can. Istas was my best project." She smiled. "Until tonight! Ezekiel would go absolutely insane if he could walk in and see us together!"

Spur lifted and she let him go. He stood and helped her up and then put his arms around her.

"Ruth, you are a special wonder. I see now how Istas stayed alive all those years. She must have learned a lot from you." He bent and kissed her lips tenderly. She whimpered and he kissed her again and then again. She pulled his head down to her breasts.

"Please?" she said and he kissed and nursed at her breasts until she murmured and he straightened.

"You must go," she said. "I don't need to worry. I come here often. If he finds me here alone, he will think I am chiding myself for some serious infraction of his rules." She smiled, reached up and kissed his lips, and then began putting on her clothes. When she was dressed she put out the lamp, and led him down the stairs.

In the darkness of the stable she reached for him and he kissed her again.

"Dear God, why couldn't I have found a man like this one to marry?" She shook her head. "I must make the best of my station. But I can always dream." She kissed Spur once more, then said a soft goodbye and watched him walk down the alley to the street.

She would see Istas tomorrow morning before the train came. She had to see the fruits of all of her efforts, and of the many hours she had spent defying Ezekiel!

Ruth turned into the back door of the house. Her life would be a little sweeter now, knowing that she had successfully defied him once more. She would be careful to stay out of his bed for the next two weeks. If she could, and what she hoped might have happened, she would enjoy the most wonderful defiance of all against Ezekiel Smith growing slowly in her womb. Yes! It had to be!

Spur McCoy walked back to the hotel. He knocked on Istas's door and found her quietly reading a stack of newspapers.

"I am so dumb!" she said as he entered. "I don't know anything about anything. I didn't even know who was president. I had no idea about how many states we have. I have so much to learn!"

Spur smiled and sat in the chair watching her. "Istas, you do not have to learn it all at once, you know."

"Did you send the telegram to St. Louis?"

"Yes, and Fleurette Leon will be expecting you, day after tomorrow."

"I am paralyzed with fear."

"You don't look it."

She jumped off the bed and he saw that she wore only her underthings, a chemise of soft silk, and frilly, knee length drawers with fancy blue ribbons and lace.

"Oh, my dress. I took it off." She sat on his lap and kissed his cheek. "Tell me about Ruth. Did you see her?"

He told her that he had talked with Ruth, and that she would come see Istas in the morning here at the hotel. "She is happy for you, delighted that you are getting away from here." He pecked her cheek and lifted her to her feet.

"Now, you did some shopping today with the money I gave you. You will need to do some more in the morning, and I'm sure Ruth will help you. Buy anything you want to, clothes, jewelry, trinkets. You have a lot of time to make up."

She took off her chemise and smiled at him, her perky, small breasts winking at him.

"One last lovemaking tonight?" she asked.

Spur shook his head. "Remember, we agreed you had to start forgetting about me. There will be plenty of young, interested men in St. Louis. Just make them wait until they marry you before you bed them. My advice. Now, into bed with you so you can shop tomorrow."

She deliberately unfastened the drawers and pulled them off, turning for his final inspection, then laughing at him she jumped between the sheets. As he tucked her in she squealed.

"I've never slept in such a fancy bed before!"

Spur McCoy kissed her and blew out the lamp.

"McCoy?"

"Yes, Istas."

"Am I pretty?"

"Istas Patterson, you are the prettiest girl in the block. I can't remember seeing a prettier girl with such wonderful soft blue eyes."

"Spur, one last time?"

He laughed, kissed her chin and then her nose and let her hug him. Then he lifted away.

"Good night, Princess. You have your whole life ahead of you. Sweet dreams."

He went out the door and closed it softly.

CHAPTER NINETEEN

SLEEPING IN WAS a luxury that Spur McCoy seldom allowed himself, but this morning he did. He woke at 5:30 as usual, turned over and went back to sleep. It was two hours later before he heard the knocking on his door. Now groggy with sleep, he staggered to the door, removed the chair from under the handle and opened the barrier.

Istas grinned at him through the crack.

"Good morning! Isn't it a glorious day! I'm heading for St. Louis this noon. Now come and take me to breakfast. I've never had breakfast in a fancy hotel before. You're not dressed?" She pushed the door open and looked in his open suitcase, grabbing brown trousers and shirt and handing them to him.

"Come on, get dressed. We can't have you going to breakfast in your short underwear, now, can we?"

McCoy laughed and so did Istas. Then she ran to him and hugged him and when she looked up at him, all of the bravado had drained from her face and she was a vulnerable waif again.

225

"How did that sound? Did I sound smart and sophisticated?"

"You sounded like a fishwife, a harpie, ordering a man around that way. And I loved it."

"Oh good." She smiled. "Now hurry. I could eat an elephant."

They had breakfast in the dining room downstairs, and she was again delighted with the linen cloth on the small table, the silverware and the delicate glassware.

She finished a poached egg and nodded. "Everything is elegant, but the food doesn't taste as good as what we fixed on the trail."

"Now you're getting the idea," Spur said. "You pay for the elegance and the service, not the food."

She had put on the blue dress she wore the night before and she looked pert and cute and determined. They were just coming back into the small lobby when someone shouted and rushed across the room.

It was Ruth Smith. The two caught each other in a hug that was rained on by tears of joy and reunion. When they stepped back Ruth rubbed at her wet cheeks.

"Sweetheart, you're beautiful!" Ruth said. "How much you have changed! There are a million things we have to talk about. First you might want to go shopping. Let me look at your things and see what you got yesterday. Do you have any money?"

"Yes, I have three hundred dollars in my reticule, and half of it is yours."

"No."

"Yes!"

"We'll talk about that later." Ruth turned to Spur and shook his hand, the only proper way for a Mormon woman to greet a man in public. She smiled at him. "It was good to see you last night."

Spur smiled. "It was good to see you too."

Ruth almost blushed thinking that he had indeed seen all of her last night. But this was Istas's day. "We'll go look at what we have now, and then go shopping. Don't expect to see us until a half hour before train time, noon, right?"

Spur nodded and they walked toward the stairs. Spur went to the stable, settled his bill and then checked out with Sheriff Derrick. The husky, medium height man stared at Spur for a minute and then nodded.

"Yep, I think it was a good thing you and the army done. Even though they lost fifteen men doing it. We shouldn't have any trouble with the Utes now for a few years. You going to be around town long?"

"Depends. Just wanted you to keep an eye on Bessie, the girl we brought back. I'm hoping her parents or the town don't give her problems because of the Indians."

"All depends."

"I had a long knuckle talk with Ezekiel Smith. I told him flat out the girl can't be persecuted or I'll rearrange his face."

Sheriff Derrick grinned. "Wanted to do that a few times myself. I'm not Mormon, but they elected me. They run a tight outfit here. I deal

227

mostly with drifters. But that Smith, he is a case. Thinks he's God almighty himself sometimes."

"Just wanted to check. You need to impress Smith about the girl, you send me a wire to St. Louis." Spur gave him the address, then stood.

"I better check at the telegraph office."

The same old telegrapher looked up as his key chattered. He was writing as the dots and dashes came over the wire. When the sound stopped, he gave the key an answering spatter of sound, then looked up.

"You Spur McCoy?"

"True."

"Got a message for you. Just a minute I'll copy it so as you can read it."

Outside the window, Spur saw two women go by. One was Istas in a pretty, soft brown dress and matching hat. She was beside Ruth and both carried packages. He watched them go into a store that announced it was the finest women's dress shop in Ogden.

"Here's your wire, Mr. McCoy." The key man handed him an envelope that had been sealed with the message inside. Usually they didn't go to that length to maintain privacy. He was about to open it when he saw another woman walk by.

Spur pushed the envelope in his pocket and hurried outside and walked quickly to catch up with the third woman who was wearing a green dress. He reached her as she paused to step down from the boardwalk into the dust of the street.

"May I assist you?" Spur asked from beside her. She looked up.

"Spur McCoy, they told me you were coming back to town. Could I bother you for a small interview? I'm always looking for good subjects for my poems."

"Hello, Candice," he said. "I'd be delighted to talk to you for as long as you want. At least until noon." She was the girl he had met on the train, the poet, the same one who had held the cocked gun to his head trying to decide if she should shoot him dead. The same sharply beautiful face with the large eyes and dark hair that billowed down, framing her face and cascading on her shoulders.

"Have you enjoyed your stay in Ogden?"

"Yes, I've written two poems, but actually I've been waiting for you. I'm doing a poem on death and I need more information by a killer."

"You've given up that line of work?"

She smiled, and took his arm as they walked across the street, lifting her skirts to miss the dirt and the occasional piles of horse droppings. At least in Washington they had street crews to clean up the droppings.

Safely on the other side she maintained her hold on his arm. "Is there anyplace in this town where a lady can get a drink?"

"The best place, in my hotel room."

"Sounds perfect to me."

"Don't you need a notebook or a pencil?"

"I have them hidden in my dress."

"You have a lot of interesting things and

places hidden by your dress," Spur said smiling.

"Why, Mr. McCoy, you are sounding absolutely sexual."

"And my professor used to tell me I wasn't communicating properly."

She laughed and a proper Mormon woman in a proper dress turned her head as they walked past.

Five minutes later Spur closed the door to his room, locked it and put the wooden chair under the door so it could not be opened from the outside even with a key.

She smiled at the precautions.

"You are an interesting man, Spur McCoy. I've been working on that poem you suggested, what was it, *Strangers On a Train?* Now I'm more interested in death." She casually began unbuttoning the top of her dress and pushed it off her shoulders until it hung at her waist. Then she lifted a soft blue chemise over her head to expose her breasts. They were as small as he had remembered, but it still gave him a lift.

"I said I was interested in death. I talked to a man once who killed his wife. He strangled her, actually, and he told me that at the first moment he got his hands around her throat, he had an erection, and when she stopped breathing and he knew he had killed her, he ejaculated in an orgasm." She looked at him. "I wish I had bigger tits to get you excited."

"A woman is a whole package, you know that. You excite me."

"Good. Now, how many men have you killed?"

"Lord, I don't know. In the army, in my job, maybe fifty, maybe a hundred."

"Any eye to eye?"

"Of course."

"Did you ever have an orgasm as you killed someone?"

"No, absolutely not! That's sick. I only kill a man or a woman when I have to, usually when they are trying to kill me. I told you about that."

"Yes."

Spur looked at his watch. It was almost eleven o'clock.

"I have to go to the train station for a while." He reached in his suitcase and brought out a bottle of bourbon whiskey. "In Mormon country I always travel with emergency supplies." He poured them both a quarter of a glassful and filled the glasses halfway with water from the china pitcher.

She sipped hers and smiled. "Now here is a man who knows how to live."

He bent and kissed her, then kissed her breasts and she lay back on the bed.

"You stay right there and don't move. I'll be back as soon as I see a friend off on the train."

"The Indian girl. Where are you sending her?"

He grinned, surprised that she knew so much about him. "Back East for an education and work. She can come back and be a big help to her people one of these days. She's only half Indian."

"Oh. Was she good making love?"

"Delicious. But not as good as you." He kissed her breasts again, chewing on them a moment, then reached for his hat, checked that his .45 was firmly in its leather home and headed for the door.

When he knocked at Istas's room, there was an immediate response. The door opened three inches and Ruth peered out.

"Oh, Mr. McCoy. We're dressing. Wait about ten minutes and then we'll need some help with the trunk."

"Trunk?"

"Of course. You don't expect a lady to travel all the way to St. Louis without a trunk? Ten minutes."

Spur went to the lobby, paid the bill on Istas's room for the night and wandered back up to the second floor. Ruth was pulling at the trunk. Istas appeared in the door, looking fresh and bright in a yellow dress with a little yellow jacket. She burst into tears and ran into his arms.

"I'll never see you again!" she wailed.

She kissed him again and again, then leaned back. "I know you'll never come to St. Louis. This Miss Leon better be nice."

Slowly she untangled herself from him and stepped back. She wiped her eyes with a linen handkerchief from her sleeve and lifted her head.

"Please take my trunk to the lobby," she said and walked away.

Ruth looked at him and smiled. "She's trying

so hard. We hid most of the money in her trunk, and sewed some in her jacket and in a small traveling bag. I shudder how much cash she has. She insisted that I take two hundred dollars. I don't know what to do with it. If Ezekiel ever found out he would snatch it away. I'll think of something." While Istas looked down the hall, Ruth reached up and kissed his lips.

"Now, we better catch up."

Spur lifted the trunk by the handles on each end, and lugged it down the stairs. In the lobby he hired a buggy to take them to the station just down the block. It was better than carrying the thing.

At the station Istas checked her purse for the ticket, then held it nervously as she looked first at Spur, then at Ruth and then down the long silvery rails.

"I'm scared!" she whispered, as she clung to Spur. He kissed her cheek.

"You're going to be fine, just great. Now don't worry about a thing. Fleurette Leon will be at the station when you get in. I'll wire her again when you leave telling her your arrival time."

Istas nodded grimly then moved to Ruth and hugged her and let some tears come.

"Ruth, you saved my life! You both saved my life! I'll never forget either one of you!"

They heard the train coming and terror blazed in Istas's eyes, then faded and she straightened her shoulders and lifted her head.

From the station someone called.

"There she is!" and a moment later Bessie ran

up and threw her arms around Istas. There was a long hug and more tears and both girls looked up.

"Istas, you saved my life! I never really thanked you. You came into that tepee and brought me out, and wrestled with the squaw and she had a knife . . . Oh, you saved my life!"

Spur saw a couple come up, hanging back a little. He went over and introduced himself.

"Are you Bessie's parents?"

"Yes, I'm Mr. Darlow, this is my wife June."

"I don't know how to thank you for bringing our little girl back from the dead," Mrs. Darlow said.

"We had talk with Ezekiel Smith, he's our bishop here in Ogden. He said everything is to be normal for Bessie. No fast marriage. We'll trust to God to keep her well until she can marry a fine young man as a first wife."

Spur nodded, told them she was strong, and she would be fine. Then he went back and stood beside Istas as the train came in.

"You've seen a hundred tains come into town, Istas."

She nodded. "But never one that I was going to leave on!" She shivered and he put his arm around her. Ruth was holding her too.

The train hissed to a stop in front of them, and Spur made sure the trunk was marked to be unloaded at St. Louis.

"You have the letter of credit and the bank deposit book?" he asked Istas. "They will let you transfer all of your money into a St. Louis bank. Tell Fleurette, she'll help you."

"Yes, I understand."

The step came down and the passengers began getting on board. She kissed Spur once more at the step, then went into the train with Ruth, who helped her find a seat. She sat next to a window and looked out and waved to Spur. She lifted the window to touch him one more time.

The train began to move and he walked along beside it, then Ruth scurried off the train and they both stood and waved as the train slowly vanished to the east.

Ruth touched Spur's arm. "Thank you, Mr. McCoy, for everything. You have been wonderful to Istas. And especially thank you for last night. I'll remember that night for as long as I live." She turned and went to join Bessie. She put her arm around Bessie as they talked. With her parents they walked out of the station.

Spur gave a big sigh and strode back to his hotel. He had one last bit of business in Ogden. He whistled as he ran up the hotel steps and into his room. He closed the door and looked at the bed. Candice lay there, naked, with the silver revolver in her right hand. She lifted it and without a word, fired.

The round went wide.

Spur dove for the bed, grabbed the cylinder as it began to turn again and stopped her from firing a second round. He jerked the gun out of her grasp and backhanded her on the side of the face, slamming her to the bed.

She yelped at the sudden pain, then rolled over and laughed.

"The look on your face! It was fantastic. I could never imagine such a look. It held raw terror, raging, sudden fear, and most interesting, disbelief. I wasn't trying to kill you. Then all of my research would be over."

Spur punched the live rounds from the .32 revolver and threw it under the bed. Then he grabbed the woman and stared at her. Slowly his anger dissolved and he kissed her and rolled on top of her on the big bed.

"Now, darling, some research about making love. Do you know the Chinese say there are one hundred and twenty-seven different positions for coitus? Do you know that?"

"If you insist, we'll try all of them this morning!"

She giggled. "Sounds tiring but instructive. Do you know all one hundred and twenty-seven positions?"

"I'm a fast learner."

The first one they tried was standing up, with her leaning out from the wall. It was half-way impossible and physically tiring. At last they gave up and collapsed on the hard wooden floor where there was no rug. By then Spur was needing his release and he pounded hard as she wailed like a wounded quail.

Later they lay on the bed.

"Show me some of your poetry," he said.

She crawled across the bed to her dress and in a skirt pocket found a slim volume that she gave to him.

He opened it and began to read somewhere in the middle.

Spur nodded and read another short poem. "It has rhyme and meter," he said. "I demand that in poetry. No sonnets?"

"Sonnets bore me, too demanding in form. No chance to break out with true creativity."

The poetry reading made him remember he had something else to read. He found his shirt and took out the unopened envelope from the telegraph office.

"What's that?" she asked.

"Orders from my boss, probably," he said. He tore open the envelope and took out the yellow telegram paper and read:

"To Spur McCoy. Ogden. Priorities. General Halleck listed them this way yesterday. #1 priority . . . Contact Henry Thompkins Paige Comstock, Virginia City, Nevada, at earliest possible date. Extreme emergency there regarding gigantic theft of silver bars and counterfeiting of replacements. Losses may be in millions of dollars. Virginia city sheriff notified you will be coming. Soonest possible response!"

The wire was signed by Fleurette Leon.

Spur took a deep breath and showed the telegram to Candice.

"Well, we have until six o'clock tonight to get in the rest of those one hundred and twenty-seven positions. Then we both can catch the train west, if you're still going that way."

"I am." She jumped up and advanced on him. "But first you owe me those hundred and twenty-six more times!"

237